FALCONDANCE

Also by Amelia Atwater-Rhodes

FALCONDANCE

Amelia Atwater-Rhodes

Delacorte Press

Published by
Delacorte Press
an imprint of
Random House Children's Books
a division of Random House, Inc.
New York

Visit us on the Web! www.randomhouse.com/teens
Educators and librarians, for a variety of teaching tools, visit us at
www.randomhouse.com/teachers

Library of Congress Cataloging-in-Publication Data

Atwater-Rhodes, Amelia.
    Falcondance / Amelia Atwater-Rhodes.
       p. cm.
    Summary: As the peaceful coexistence of the avian and serpiente realms
becomes increasingly precarious, nineteen-year-old Nicias, heir to the ancient
and powerful falcon realm, learns some lessons about the past that will shape the
future of their shared world.
    ISBN 0-385-73194-9 (trade)   ISBN 0-385-90334-0 (GLB)
    [1. Falcons—Fiction. 2. Self-realization—Fiction. 3. Birds—Fiction.
4. Snakes—Fiction. 5. Fantasy.] I. Title.
    PZ7.A8925Fal 2005
    [Fic]—dc22

                                                                    2004023890

The text of this book is set in 12-point Loire.

Book design by Jason Zamajtuk

Printed in the United States of America

September 2005

10 9 8 7 6 5 4 3

BVG

Falcondance
*is dedicated to Jesse Sullivan,
to Montreal and Maryland and New York,
and the road trips thereto that allowed me to finish editing this book.*

shm'Ahnmik'nesera
Mehay'hena-ke-Jesse Sullivan
ke-a'Montreal'Maryland'tih-a'la'varl'ban'ciab'kaen

*Also,
I give thanks to:
Kylesito, my inspiration for Nicias;
Ollie, my inspiration for more than I could possibly list on a page; RC Carpenter, who
knows my world nearly as well as I do; Seán Nikolas, for his sharp eyes and quick mind;
and Jodi, an excellent editor, who really should have had her name in here before this.*

ke'ke
la-varl'teska-a
a'Nicias'kayla-Kylesito
a'las'hena'kayla-Ollie-ke'ke-RC Carpenter-ke-heah'lo'la
eh'ak'ysfeth'la'SeánNikolas'kaen'rait'tansa'he'gase
de'patase'la'Jodi

*Finally, credit must go to:
Professor Feldman, who taught me to love philosophy;
Michael Rubin, who is the only instructor with whom I would ever study politics;
and of course Susan Cocalis–and Latte–for simply being incredible.*

maen'ciab-varl'wim-a
de'raviheah'la'Feldman-ke-varl'toth'o'jaes'heah
Michael Rubin-ke-ne'mnan
Susan Cocalis-ke'ke-Latte-ke-hena'hena

To knowledge, inspiration and creation
a'heah-a'kayla-a'Mehay'hena

a'le-Ahnleh

THE SHAPE

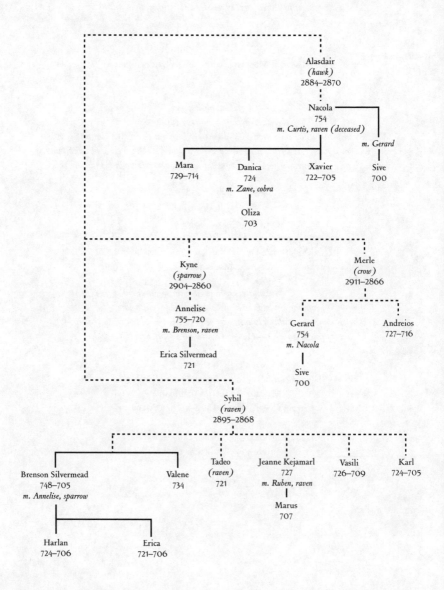

Alasdair
(hawk)
2884–2870

Nacola
754
m. Curtis, raven (deceased)

m. Gerard

Mara
729–714

Danica
724
m. Zane, cobra

Xavier
722–705

Sive
700

Oliza
703

Kyne
(sparrow)
2904–2860

Merle
(crow)
2911–2866

Annelise
755–720
m. Brenson, raven

Gerard
754
m. Nacola

Andreios
727–716

Erica Silvermead
721

Sive
700

Sybil
(raven)
2895–2868

Brenson Silvermead
748–705
m. Annelise, sparrow

Valene
734

Tadeo
(raven)
721

Jeanne Kejamarl
727
m. Ruben, raven

Vasili
726–709

Karl
724–705

Marus
707

Harlan
724–706

Erica
721–706

Dashed lines indicate not only a lapse of several generations, but also an indirect relation.

SHIFTERS

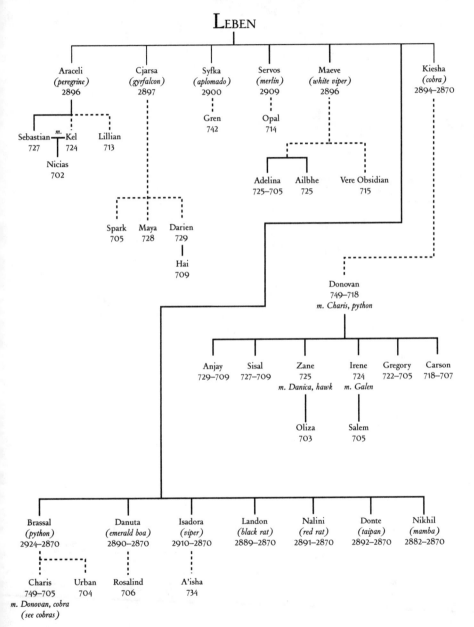

PROLOGUE

*H*ERE WE ARE, *among the lucky ones who live in times of peace, in times of hope and dreams and laughter. Here we are, in the glimmering Wyvern's Court.*

Yet my dreams are not of the slate walks and marble plaza of my home. They are not of the velvet floor of the nest, of the exotic serpents' dance or the haunting melodies that can be heard at all times from the southern hills. Nor are they of the glint of sunlight on soaring wings, or the smooth hum of avian voices.

Ahnmik. That is the city of which I dream. Ahnmik, the falcon land of which I have learned so much and so little all at once. My parents refuse to speak of the land in which they were born. They have accepted this avian-serpiente world as the only one they will ever have.

But Lillian has painted my dreams with images of a city that glitters with magic. She speaks hesitantly of her homeland, because she knows that my parents' crimes will forever keep me from the island, but each word twines around some part of my heart.

I will always be loyal to Wyvern's Court, but how can I fail to think about the tall white arches that are said to be created not by any creature's hand, but by pure strength of will? How can my nights not hold roads that sing a melody no voice or instrument can produce?

Ahnmik.

Of course I have learned of the city's namesake, the god so powerful that even those who laugh at myths fear to call his name in vain. Ahnmik is shown in art as a white falcon, diving through sky and sea alike, and his domain is power. It is control. It is magic.

The serpents of Wyvern's Court worship Anhamirak, the goddess who grants free will, and they fear Ahnmik. The falcons, however, believe that Ahnmik has a gentle side, just as the serpents' Anhamirak has a violent one. Ahnmik is the one who can grant sleep, and silence. When whatever nightmares plague my mother's sleep have become too much, I have heard her call to Ahnmik—and I have seen my father's look of horror.

Long ago, the serpiente and the falcons made up one civilization. They worked and worshipped together, until something caused the two sides to clash, and the falcons were driven out of the land. Serpiente history books say that Ahnmik's followers practiced black magic, endangering the falcons and the serpiente, and were exiled for that reason.

Lillian always shies away from the subject of the conflict, saying only that history is easily distorted by years, and by the teller.

As a falcon raised in Wyvern's Court, I do not know what I believe. I try to base my decisions on facts, but what facts are left from a fight that occurred thousands of years ago?

I ramble. I find that I do that more of late, as I think of things I will never have and never know. I am posted in Wyvern's Court as one of the princess's personal guards, a lofty rank of which I am proud. But contentment . . . that is beyond my grasp, drifting away as though in a gust of Anhamirak's storm winds.

Anhamirak's domain is also of spilled blood.

Of fire that sears.

Of tempests that drown.

Beauty and light and passion are hers, but simplicity she can never grant.

Nicias Silvermead
Wyvern of Honor

CHAPTER 1

M Y BREATH STILLED for an instant as I watched the blade slice a hairsbreadth from the fair skin of Oliza Shardae Cobriana, nineteen-year-old princess of Wyvern's Court.

"Relax." The reassurance came from the cobra beside me, Oliza's only cousin, Salem Cobriana. "I've seen her perform this blade dance a hundred times in the nest." He shot me an amused look as he added, "With dulled blades."

The dagger went up once more as Oliza sank to the ground, closing her eyes and bowing her head before clapping her hands behind her back to catch the weapon one final time.

Members of the audience approached the dais, where Oliza remained perfectly poised as her fans placed flowers and small gifts in front of her. This had by no means been her debut, but it had been her first time performing the *jaes'falnas*—the blade dances that her parents had almost forbidden her to learn.

After seeing her perform, and seeing just how sharp the performance blades were, part of me wished they had.

A serpiente dancer could, and often did, risk her life in pursuit of her trade. Oliza Shardae Cobriana, however, was not just a dancer, but heir to two thrones. Her mother, Danica Shardae, was the avian Tuuli Thea, and her father, Zane Cobriana, was Diente to the serpiente. Oliza's reign would mean the merging of two monarchies that had, until our parents' generation, been at war for thousands of years. But first Oliza had to choose her king, a decision for which all of Wyvern's Court waited anxiously, and one that had led many a young man to try to court her.

Oliza smiled at me, meeting my gaze just long enough to express her exhilaration before a petite golden-haired girl managed to slip through the crowd to stand next to me. Surprise washed over Oliza's face when she saw the unexpected guest, and she quickly came toward us.

"I can see why your parents objected to your studying these dances," Sive Shardae remarked, admiration clear in her voice despite her chastising words. "My mother would never have allowed it." Sive was three years younger than Oliza, but was the younger sister of Oliza's mother. Though still very avian in her mannerisms, she had made a point of stepping away from her avian tutors and spending more and more time with the serpiente in the past few years, learning their ways. She had not bridged the gap between the two cultures as completely as Oliza had, but that she was here at all spoke volumes. Twenty years earlier, a young avian woman would not have been permitted to walk alone through the market—much less watch the "scandalous" dances of the serpiente.

She's not quite alone, I thought as I scanned the crowd. Sive's alistair, Prentice, was standing just beyond the edge of

Oliza's audience, his gaze never leaving his charge. I watched him carefully, for out of this group, he was always the most likely to cause a disturbance.

The raven had made his distrust of serpents very clear, and he became especially irritable when Sive insisted on spending time with the dancers. Serpiente hugged and flirted casually with almost everyone, but Sive's alistair bristled at having to tolerate that kind of attention being paid to his pair bond.

Salem, leaving on his way back to the dancers' nest, greeted the raven politely. Prentice nodded curtly at the serpiente. He had argued with Salem in the past, but that day they managed to walk by each other without raised voices.

Progress, at least.

"Ridiculous," Oliza said to Sive, oblivious to the frosty moment between the two men. "No one has died performing a blade dance in sixty years."

Sive looked at me as if seeking reason, before realizing that Oliza was teasing her. Sive's scandalized expression made her appear even younger than her seventeen years.

It made me think back to when I had been a child and my parents had first brought me to see Wyvern's Court. I remembered the day fifteen years before as vividly as if it was playing before me that moment.

I stood beside my parents, trying to mimic their careful attention as they watched Oliza and her family. My mother, Kel Silvermead, was captain of the Royal Flight, one of the elite guards who protected Oliza's mother, the Tuuli Thea; my father was her second-in-command. Their attention never strayed from their charges, but mine shifted momentarily to the rolling hills and gentle valley where architects had been laboring for years.

Oliza's grandmother, Nacola Shardae, was there, with a nurse next to her holding the sleepy infant Sive. Salem, exactly twenty months older than Oliza, suddenly pulled away from his mother and father to whisper something in the princess's ear.

Without warning, both royal children took off down the hill. Adults tried to follow, but Oliza and Salem thought it was a great game to hide in the empty market stalls from their parents and guards, deaf to all the worried shouts.

✳✳✳

Oliza touched my arm, startling me from my memories.

"You look skies away," she said softly. I realized suddenly that the crowd had dispersed.

"I was thinking about our first day here," I said, though I knew that wasn't enough of an explanation. It was not my habit to let my mind wander—not when I was with Oliza. I looked around uneasily and tried to account for the missing minutes.

"I hardly remember it," Oliza admitted, not noticing my disquiet as she led us from the market. This was our ritual; we walked and talked until we reached the woods, and then, beyond the edges of the court, we changed shape and spread wing. "We were so young. I just remember you finding me, after I got lost in the woods. No matter what kind of trouble I got into, it seemed you were always there."

I didn't say aloud that I could still find the exact tree beneath which she had been cowering, though it was true. My parents were the only people I knew who had never been surprised by my memory.

Of course, my mother had replied once, when questioned by my teacher about my fast progress. *He is a falcon.*

She had never said those exact words to me, but they always hung in the air, every time I shot past my peers in class. I had begun training with the royal guards when I was nine, while others my age were still studying . . . or playing. Many of the children had been wary of me, a falcon in their midst. They knew the falcons' history of black magic, and they knew that the falcons had sided with the avians—against the serpiente—during the war.

And none of them liked being around someone who made them feel stupid.

By fifteen, I had become a Wyvern of Honor, one of the dozen members of Oliza's personal guard, and that position meant more to me than any teacher's praise. Again, my parents had been proud, but not surprised; standing side by side on the street, we looked nothing alike, but I would always be their son.

Before I had even been born, my mother's falcon magic had given her the visage of a sparrow, and my father's had made him a crow. But their power was bound now. That was why my pale golden hair did not match my parents'; my mother frowned at the way it lightened to silver in the front. Beneath my hair, my feathers were blue-violet. When I grew the wings of my Demi form, the markings were peregrine. My parents' magic had altered their forms irrevocably, but genetics had made me the child of what they had been: falcons.

"Nicias?" This time Oliza sounded worried. "Is something wrong? You've seemed so distracted lately."

For the past several nights, my dreams had been filled

with the white towers of Ahnmik, and my nightmares had been stained by cobras trapped in ice and whispering voices I strained to hear, which made me stumble in the cold darkness.

"I haven't been sleeping well," I said, not elaborating. Oliza had her own burdens. She didn't need my troubles. "I must just be a little tired."

"Too tired to fly?" she asked, her tone light but her expression more serious. "I'd like to get out of here for a while."

Unspoken between us were the many reasons she usually asked me to stay beside her instead of one of her many other guards.

I was only one year younger than she was, and we had grown up together. I was also the only person in the court who didn't call her Wyvern, a nickname she hated but would probably never shake.

The serpents in her guard could never follow her in the skies, and I knew that Oliza disliked flying with the pureblood sparrows, crows and ravens that filled the avian side of town. She preferred to fly with a falcon, someone who not only could match her pace, but also was just as out of place among the avians and serpiente as she was. But the most important reason, the one she would never speak aloud, was that she preferred to fly with someone who wasn't courting her—and never could.

Soon the serpiente were going to stop treading lightly around her half-avian parentage and start pursuing her, and the avians were going to start panicking. I saw that Oliza was always cautious not to show more favor to one male friend than any other now.

With me, she never had to worry. She would be queen of

the avians and serpiente, and so she must have one of them as her king. And I . . .

I was a falcon, and my parents had cautioned me many times about the dangers of choosing an avian or serpiente pair bond, regardless of how I might feel. The other falcons would never allow such a union.

Oliza and I would always be friends.

Once we reached the woods, Oliza stretched her arms above her head and sighed. In the afternoon sunlight, she was beautiful in the most uncanny way. Her black hair glistened with red highlights; the feathers that grew on her nape ranged in color from deep copper to rust. Her eyes were as golden as the rising sun and were surrounded by long, dark lashes.

And here, out of sight of the rest of the world, she shifted form.

Her serpent body was as flexible as a whipcord, its scales the same color as her hair—black with glints of red and gold. A ruff of avian feathers grew across the hood, spreading onto the powerful wings that unfurled from her back.

Wyvern. She cut through the air like lightning.

I followed her as a peregrine falcon, shrieking a cry of triumph to the sky that Oliza answered with a call too musical to be called a hawk's screech.

Absolutely, without compromise, unavailable.

I knew it; she knew it. It made our relationship safe.

We landed on the shore of a distant sea, hours away from Wyvern's Court. Oliza's talons dug furrows in the loose sand before she returned to her human form, shaking her ruffled hair out of her face. We had passed high above many human villages, too distant for their inhabitants' weak eyes to perceive Oliza's form as unusual.

"Sometimes I consider just flying and flying until I find someplace I've never even heard of," Oliza confided, her face still flushed from the flight. "Then I would land, take my human form, and live there the rest of my life."

I laughed a little. "Humble goals for the princess of two worlds."

She joined in my laughter. "I must seem terribly spoiled. Arami of the serpiente, and heir to the Tuuli Thea, and I want something else completely. No one's ever happy with what they have, I suppose."

"True," I answered, thinking of my own dreams of flying and flying . . . until I reached the white shores of Ahnmik, an island that lay in a sea I did not know.

Time passed in companionable silence as we sat on the beach, waiting for the tide to come in and the waves to lap across our toes.

I found that when I looked into the sea just the right way, the ripples where the sun hit the water looked like writing. I mentioned it to Oliza, but she just shook her head.

"Not from this angle," she answered. She leaned toward me, black hair brushing my shoulder. I caught the faint fragrance of almond, a scent she often wore, and had a momentary desire to wrap an arm about her waist.

I fought down the impulse.

It was impossible to count how many times over the past few years I had been tempted to say or do something just as stupid as putting an arm around her now would be.

Finding nothing in the waves, Oliza shook her head again. "I think perhaps you've had too much sun, Nicias Silvermead."

"Perhaps."

She looked at me strangely for a moment, maybe hearing something in my voice—a hint of longing for all things impossible.

"We should get back," she said as she stood. "We'll be late for dinner as it is. Again."

I pushed myself to my feet, brushing sand from my clothing. "Race you?" I challenged her, to break the tension.

Her eyes lit as she teased, "Do you need a head start?"

"Hardly," I answered haughtily, which earned me a handful of sand in the chest.

"Fine, then."

She took off like an arrow in flight, gaining air on me almost immediately. The lead she had now would diminish later; Oliza was always the faster flier at first, but she paced herself poorly, and during a longer flight I was almost always able to overtake her.

I let her pull ahead, not pressing my speed yet, and heard her challenging cry as the wind carried it back to me. The air was clear, and I kept an eye on her, but did not fret about the distance between us; I did not fear for the wyvern's safety, not in these skies.

One thing I would never regret about being a falcon was flight: the warmth of the sun even as it was quickly sinking in the west; the ground rushing by, far below; and the steady beat of wings. I complained about my falcon blood sometimes, but never would I complain about having a falcon's power in my wings. I let out a whoop of joy as my sleek feathered body cut through the air.

CHAPTER 2

RIVERS, MOUNTAINS, fields and trees stretched out below me, their contours forming complex patterns I could never quite follow. And around it all danced the wind, moving east and west, dragging the clouds above and the leaves below.

That day it seemed almost as if I could see the lines as they formed, rippled, moved and reset. If I could only pause to look at them—

And suddenly I lost the rhythm not only of the Earth but of the sky and felt myself falling as fast as a stone toward the ground that seemed to rush up to catch me.

With too much effort I twisted in the air, changing the fall to a dive. A natural peregrine falcon can stoop at two hundred miles an hour as it dives for its prey, and I used every ounce of that ability now.

When I reached the ground, I slammed into human form, my heart pounding, breath labored, palms on cool dirt below me as I fought to keep from retching.

What had happened?

One doesn't *forget* to fly any more than one forgets to

breathe. I could think of a million things and never miss a wing stroke. So what had happened?

I tried to stand and found that I was trembling not with shock, but with pure exhaustion.

I caught my breath as my gaze fell upon a pair of eyes the color of blue opals. There seemed to be nothing beyond them—no forest, no sky—just those icy gems looking at me from some world beyond this one as if startled by my presence. The air seemed frozen, and I recoiled—

Then the eyes I saw were not blue, but liquid silver. They regarded me with curiosity, and a woman's voice said gently, "Nicias—"

Mercury bled into garnet as her silver gaze gave way to twin pools of blood, still as death, and furious at my intrusion—

Get out.

The words shot through my mind, the woman's voice familiar but at the same time unlike any I had ever heard.

***

Again I was on the ground, as if that third woman had shoved me away. Illusion, hallucination—I didn't know what to call the visions. That final gaze had looked like a cobra's. I pressed my cheek to the rough bark of the tree, trying in vain to figure out what was going on.

Oliza must have arrived home by now and hurried to dinner, either expecting me to follow or thinking I was already there. Again, I had left her unguarded when it was my duty to protect her. There was no room for a weakness that left me unable to do that.

Another, more chilling thought occurred to me. What if Oliza had been under this spell, too?

I pushed myself up, forcing my limbs to stop shaking. I needed to find Oliza. I changed shape and pressed into the skies, cursing the lethargy that seemed to make my wings heavy and awkward.

What had happened to me?

I knew one person who might be able—and willing—to explain. Lillian. But I wouldn't be able to speak to her until later that night.

Now I had to find Oliza. I went straight to the Rookery and was relieved to find her safe in the dining area. Her cheeks were still flushed from the flight, so I could not have been out as long as I had thought. She shot me an amused, triumphant glance that said she would needle me later for having finally lost a race to her. Then she politely turned her attention back to the crow with whom she had been speaking.

My mother had been at the Hawk's Keep with Danica Shardae the past few days, but she did not leave the Tuuli Thea to greet me, or even to ask why I was late. My father was engaged in a conversation with the Diente, Zane Cobriana, and looked up only long enough to frown at my tardiness.

I would hear about it later, but duty had always come first to both of my parents.

Oliza *did* walk over to me, which prompted Gretchen— the python who led the Wyverns—to do the same.

"Silvermead—"

Oliza's friendly voice cut off what would probably have been a chastisement of me. "Next time we race, I'll give you a head start," she offered. To Gretchen, she added, "You can hardly blame him for being late when I'm the one who kept him, can you?"

If only that were the truth.

Dinner, despite the presence of the Tuuli Thea, the Diente, most of the royal family and a few members of the court, was a relatively informal event. I would have liked to talk to Oliza more, but most of her attention was dedicated to her parents and her more insistent suitors.

A crow named Marus pulled Oliza aside when we were through. Though he had been born in the Hawk's Keep, Marus had moved here with his family when he was ten, and he had been courting Oliza with all the careful charm of an avian gentleman for the past few years. He was among the most tolerable of her suitors, and tried to be open-minded despite his very conservative upbringing, but I doubted he would ever care to watch Oliza perform one of the serpents' dances.

In some rumors he was named the next king, but those were rumors started by gossips who knew nothing. Oliza spoke of Marus the same way she spoke of many of her suitors—with some fondness, but nothing more.

"If you have the time," Marus said, any nervousness flawlessly hidden behind a shield of avian self-control, "I was wondering if you might like to walk with me this evening."

"Unfortunately, I've promised my night to the dancers," she answered. "But if you would like to escort me to the nest, I wouldn't mind the company."

Marus hesitated, as I had known he would. The nest was located on the southern hills of Wyvern's Court, in an area that was primarily serpiente. Although avians were not banned from the area, they were somewhat out of place.

Wyvern's Court was not yet a perfect blend of the two worlds. Many serpents were just as hesitant to walk the northern hills as Marus was to walk the southern ones. I believed, however, that every generation would step farther across the valley. Many others of my generation would make the effort specifically for Oliza.

Then Marus nodded, as if he had weighed the benefits of walking with Oliza against the unease he still felt around serpents and found the former worth the latter.

I followed them to the doorway, then saw Oliza take Marus's arm and felt a pang of envy.

"It kills you to watch her walk away with him, doesn't it?" The soft voice startled me so much that I jumped, though by then I should have been used to Lillian's quiet coming and going.

I turned to Lily with a sharp look, then regretted it as her gaze dropped.

"I'm sorry," she said. "I just hate to see that expression on your face, knowing that she either doesn't see it, or doesn't want to."

"It's better that way," I said.

"Better . . . yes," she echoed, the words hollow. "I hope this evening is your own, at least. I need to talk to you."

"I'm not on duty tonight." Oliza never took a guard to the dancer's nest. Looking more closely at Lily, I realized that there was sorrow in her gray-blue eyes. "Is something wrong?"

Lily lived in constant fear of what might happen if someone discovered that she was not the simple raven most people saw when they looked at her.

I had tried many times to convince her to tell Oliza the truth, but she had refused.

Perhaps you are right, she had said once when pressed, *and your Oliza would never betray me to the rest of her people, but I cannot afford to take that chance. A falcon will always be an outsider here, someone to fear and hate and avoid.*

She had apologized almost instantly, but her words had still cut deeply. Too true. At least I was familiar in these lands, the son of two respected members of the Royal Flight, and one of the princess's elite guards. Otherwise, I doubted my living here would be tolerated.

I was not prepared for Lily's answer.

"I've just received a summons from Araceli," she said. *Araceli.* It was always jarring to hear Lily say, without hesitation, a name my own parents never dared utter. The heir to the falcon Empress was my father's mother—and she had disowned and exiled him before I had even been born. It took a moment for me to register the rest of Lily's statement: "I'll be returning home within the next few days."

Lily had never pretended that she would be in Wyvern's Court forever, but the suddenness of this hit me like a shock of cold water.

"Will I see you again?" My voice sounded faraway to me. I knew what the answer would be.

"Probably not," she replied. "I was granted this leave to see Wyvern's Court because I lost someone very dear to me in Araceli's service, and she believed I should be given some time of my own. You must agree that two years was a very generous reprieve. Now I have responsibilities to which I must return."

I did agree, and I did understand. I just didn't know what to say now. When Lily and I had first met, she had been like a window to a land that had always fascinated me. In the past two years, she had become one of my few friends in Wyvern's Court. Besides Oliza, Lily was the one person who looked at me not as a falcon, but simply as Nicias.

"Nicias!" Her sharp tone made me jump. "Have you been this distant all day?"

"I'm sorry."

"What happened?" I did not want to burden her with the events of my day, but before I could change the subject, she caught my hand in hers. "Nicias, you aren't normally distractible, yet I can see that it's taking an effort for you to keep your attention on me. You look exhausted. Please, talk to me."

I took a deep breath and tried to focus. "It's probably just fatigue. I've had nightmares the last several nights, and haven't been sleeping well." I shrugged. "I keep thinking about things that happened years ago and completely losing track of time."

I tried haltingly to describe what had happened during my flight with Oliza, and watched her face turn pale.

"Nicias ... have you spoken to your parents about this yet?"

I shook my head.

"Que'le'kaheah'hekna-a'tair'ferat'jarka-takmu!" Though I was not quite fluent, I had studied the old language for years; what little I could understand of the string of profanity Lily spat out made it clear why my tutors had not taught me the rest. "You have to tell them," she asserted, in a more familiar language. "They might have left Ahnmik, but they're falcon-born, and they deserve to know. I need—I need to speak to my lady."

Despite the fear I could hear in her voice, she sounded excited. "Wait," I called as she turned to leave.

She darted back and kissed my cheek. "Go, speak to Kel now. I must speak with your father's mother."

I winced as Lillian evoked my lineage again.

My hand lost its grip on Lily as she shifted shape and a raven shot into the air. Even though I knew that the bird I saw was a product of magic, an illusion, I could never make out the peregrine falcon she said was her true second form.

I watched the raven disappear on the horizon, fearing that I would never see her again or have a chance to say goodbye.

Suddenly I heard her voice, as clear as if she was standing beside me. *Do not worry, Nicias. I have easier ways of speaking to my lady than flying all the way back to the island. I will stay near, and you will see me again, soon.*

Magic? Lily had always been discreet with her power. But now she had given me a taste of what I had never had . . . and had assumed I never would.

I took my own falcon form, obeying her command to seek my parents. An idea, a strange hope, was beginning to take shape in my mind, but I didn't know whether it was a combination of dreams and fatigue or a reasonable conclusion.

CHAPTER 3

M Y MOTHER WAS still deep in conversation with the Diente and the Tuuli Thea when I returned to the Rookery, and even if I had been bleeding to death, I would have
hesitated to interrupt. Fortunately my father noticed me
idling there and excused himself from the others.

"What's wrong?"

I hardly knew how to begin. I could not use Lily's command as an explanation, since my father would not even know
who she was. I had known that my parents would never trust
a falcon as my friend, and so had never mentioned her to them.

"Something strange happened to me today, on my way
back with Oliza."

"Strange how?" he prompted when I hesitated, hating to
trouble my father.

"I was flying behind Oliza, and suddenly I . . . fell." I
struggled for words that made sense. "I was watching the
ground, and then it was like I forgot where I was. I barely
managed to land safely, and then I saw something; at least, I
think I did. Something that wasn't there."

Sometime during the speech, my mother had joined us at the door, perhaps to see what was keeping my father. He did not seem too disturbed by my words, but my mother's expression was grave.

"Has anything else happened?" she asked. "Strange dreams or nightmares?"

I nodded.

"Vemka'mehka'Ahnleh," she swore under her breath. "Rei, say what you must to Zane and Danica. I'm taking our son home."

"Kel—"

"They'll understand; they're parents, too," she argued, never raising her voice from a fierce whisper. "Nicias, let's go. We need to talk."

I followed her from the Rookery to our home on the northern hills. My father caught up with us by wing as we mounted the two steps to the doorway.

Both my parents normally conducted themselves like older-generation avians, controlling their expressions and their voices, but right then they both looked tense and worried. I could not remember another time when my parents had excused themselves from our monarchs to attend to *me;* their doing so now, when I was almost twenty years old, could not be a good sign.

My mother began to pace in our living room. The restless action was so unlike her that it ripped the question from me: "What is happening to me?"

"When your father and I were exiled from the island," my mother began slowly, "the Lady Araceli, heir to the falcon Empress Cjarsa, bound us into the forms we had used to hide among the avians when we first left Ahnmik. She stripped us of our falcon forms, and took away our magic." She looked to my father for support as she summarized the tale I knew, then moved on. "As you know, falcon magic—*jaes'Ahnmik*—is so powerful that the serpiente and avians have feared it for thousands of years. That magic runs very strongly in the royal house of Ahnmik, where your father's mother is heir. It also ran very strongly in me. After our magic was bound . . ."

She swore again in the falcons' language, trailing off with a whispered prayer of *"Varl'falmay."* Help me with this.

"That magic should never have showed in you," she continued, "not with both of your parents locked from it. But everything you have been experiencing lately I have seen in others, when they first discovered their power."

Chills ran down my spine. I had suspected something like this from the moment Lily had told me to go to my parents.

"Even if I do have this magic, why does it frighten you so much?" I asked. "I would never use it to harm anyone; you *know* I would never use it against Wyvern's Court."

"I know," she said, shaking her head. "But I worry it will use *you*."

"Kel," my father finally spoke, putting a hand on my mother's arm to still her pacing, "what if all this worrying is premature? We both left the island when we were younger than Nicias is now, and neither of us ever had a problem."

She looked at him as if he had gone mad, then sighed, her gaze turning distant. "Sebastian of Ahnmik . . ." He winced when she called him by the name he had once used, as Araceli's son. *"Sebastian* would have passed the four summers Trial without effort. He was royal blood, after all—"

"As is Nicias—"

"It doesn't matter." My mother spoke over my father's protests. "I never knew Sebastian. But I can say with certainty that he had years of training before coming to avian lands. I passed the Trials when I was seven; it was another nine years before I fled. And both of us stole avian forms within a month of arriving, which kept the magic in check until Araceli bound it. Neither of us has the ability to teach our son, or to bind him."

"What do you propose we do, Kel?" my father asked, his voice strained. "I know the danger as well as you do. What I don't know is the solution."

"I might not have been raised on Ahnmik studying this magic," I said in the ensuing silence, struggling to keep my voice respectful despite my irritation, "but I'm not an idiot and I'm not a child. Would one of you please speak *to* me, instead of arguing as if I am not here?"

My mother looked at me for long moments, then said to my father, "We have to send him to Araceli, ask her to—"

"No." My father's response was swift. "Sending him to my mother would be madness. The only reason I got out when I was young was that Syfka convinced Araceli to let me spend some time off the island, and taught me to force-change so I would be able to hide from her—"

"Isn't it madness to keep him here?" my mother demanded. "I've known that this might happen from the time he was three and I saw the first silver in his hair. I assure you, I have considered every option."

All that time, and she had never told me, warned me? My father spoke before I could.

"Have you considered that we are both outlaws, Kel? There is no assurance that Araceli will even agree to see Nicias, or that she won't execute him on the spot as the son of traitors. If she *does* see him, *and* agrees to teach him . . . it will be because she sees herself in his face, a pure-blood falcon with his beauty still intact, unmarred by a crow's features. I am my mother's only child, but I am dead to her. In our son, she may see a villain or she may see her *heir*. If she agrees to teach him, it will mean she has no intention of letting him go."

"She won't force him to stay," my mother said. "Nicias will be powerful. If she does not bind his magic, she will need to teach him, and once she teaches him, he will have the strength to resist her."

"I'm not worried she'll force him," he said, though his voice had the tone of one who had given up.

Finally, *finally*, he turned to me, as if realizing that I deserved to have some part in this conversation about my life.

"Nicias, Ahnmik's magic is powerful enough to destroy its user, if he cannot control it. Most falcons begin to study almost as soon as they can walk, just to keep it from killing them." His voice was level, as controlled as any avian's, but I could see the effort that control took. "Most royal-blood falcons use their magic innately, and so it may be with you. . . . But your mother is right. As a child, even I was given exercises to help me focus my mind and keep me from losing myself in the magic."

"Rei—"

He cut my mother off with a look. She sighed, but allowed him to continue.

"It may be that this fall today was a fluke, caused by your magic waking when you weren't expecting it. It may be that this will be all, that your magic has been crippled by the bonds put on your mother and me, and it will never grow stronger; that would probably be for the best. Or, your power may simply have been hidden all these years, and now it will show as true as any falcon's. If it does grow, you may be able to control it effortlessly—or you may not." He drew a deep breath and then continued. "If you can't, it will destroy you. It will numb your body and mind, until it drives you into what is called *shm'Ecl*. There are rooms on Ahnmik filled with those who have succumbed to it, those who could not learn to control their power. They are neither alive nor dead, neither awake nor asleep. . . ."

His voice wavered, his gaze turning distant. He shook himself, as if to clear away something foul that clung to his skin.

"There are two people I know who are powerful enough to bind a falcon's magic," my mother finished for him. "The Empress herself, and her heir, the Lady Araceli of Ahnmik."

"My grandmother."

She nodded.

My father spoke again. "My mother is a devious woman, Nicias, not a kind one. If you go to her, I don't know what will happen. I worry . . . I worry you won't return." I could not tell whether he feared that his mother would kill me, or something worse. Did he really think anyone could convince me to abandon my home?

He added, "But you may be in just as much danger staying here. I don't know. But as you've said, Nicias, you're not a child; your mother and I can't make this choice for you."

At once I regretted those words, because now I *wanted* to be a child again, so that I would not need to face this decision. Stay here, where I might be fine or I might decline into madness, or go to Ahnmik, where I might be executed or I might finally see and study in the city that had haunted my dreams?

"I need some time to think," I said. "If it's true that today might have been a fluke, can we wait, and make this decision after we see whether it happens again?"

"Maybe," my mother answered. "But if that is your

choice, I would recommend you ask for leave from Oliza's guard for a while, until we know whether your magic will interfere with your duty. And, Nicias, please try to avoid activities that could be dangerous if you were . . . distracted."

Distracted. I remembered falling in the woods, and the time I had lost after watching Oliza dance, when anything could have happened to her without my noticing. Yes, my mother's suggestions made sense.

"Tonight we should all get some sleep," my father said. "Fatigue doesn't help anyone keep alert—or make decisions."

✳✳✳

I tried to obey, but as I tossed and turned in bed, images from the day and visions spawned by my parents' words kept shifting through my mind.

When I finally did drift into sleep, those visions invaded my nightmares, twisting around everything. I found myself locked inside black ice, frozen and still, unable to escape—

Garnet cobra's eyes, staring at me with fury. A cobra's fangs, bared and glistening with poison—

Ice, rippling with white lines like a million silver scars; it cracked and shrieked and bled—

My prince, whispered a voice—the same one that had shouted at me in the woods, angrily telling me to go away. *You are too brilliant for this dark land. . . .*

Then Oliza stood before me. She touched my hand and then there was fire—

I scrambled away, choking on the smell of burned flesh, and slid on the ice. A black cobra coiled around me, the scales cold against my skin.

Why am I drawn to your dreams? she asked. *What vows bind you to me?*

"You're a cobra," I managed to whisper. "I am sworn to the royal house."

My prince, do you think me a fool? she snarled.

Abruptly the cobra became a python. It wrapped around my body, binding my arms and constricting my chest until I struggled to breathe.

You are *the royal house. Your royal blood infects this land like a virus—*

✳✳✳

I woke, gasping and coughing as I tried to draw air into my body. For long moments I could only feel the cold coils of the serpent, pulling me back.

Finally I became aware of a gentler voice.

"Nicias, Nicias, come back to me," Lily was whispering. Her hands were warm on mine, which made me realize that I was shivering.

I forced myself to open my eyes, disoriented by her presence as much as by the dream.

"You cried out, with your magic," she said. "I felt you fall, felt you go cold—did you speak to your parents?"

"I—" The effort of trying to speak made me cough again. My ribs felt bruised.

As if reading my mind, Lily placed one hand gently on my chest. "There isn't too much damage," she said after a moment. Warmth seemed to spread from her touch, dispelling the lingering chill from the nightmare. "I was so frightened—"

The door opened.

"I thought I heard—" My mother broke off, looking from me to Lily and then back to me. Her obvious conclusion, though false, made me blush and pull away from Lily slightly.

Lily didn't look embarrassed or bother to explain who she was or why she was there. Her fear for me became anger as she demanded, "You left him alone? The evening after his magic awakened, you let him sleep with no one near to pull him back?"

"I didn't realize there was anyone in the area who—"

"You and your pair bond hid for years among the avians," Lily snapped. "You of all people must know that there are at least half a dozen of us in the area—"

"And who exactly are you?" my mother finally asked.

Lily drew a deep breath, visibly struggling to control her temper. "A woman who cares about your son," she said softly. "I would think that is something we share."

My father joined my mother in the doorway. He glanced at her questioningly, and she shook her head slightly.

"Nicias, I can fly with you to Ahnmik if you would like, to show you the way and keep you safe from your magic over the open seas," Lily said.

My father cleared his throat, attracting our attention. "Have you already made your decision, then, Nicias?"

"What other choice is there?" Lily asked. "I felt his magic clear across Wyvern's Court. Even among your avians and serpents, you will hear people speak tomorrow of their nightmares from this evening. Maybe you don't have the power to sense his magic pressing him, but I can tell you without doubt, if he does not begin studying the *jaes'Ahnmik*, he will fall within the week."

Still my parents hesitated, as if they were hearing different words than I was, less frightening ones.

"You would allow him to stay here, knowing..." Lily let

out an angry cry. "How selfish can you be? You know that he will not survive here. He needs—enough!" She ran her hands through her hair, drawing my attention to the tangles in the blond strands. I realized then that she must have come here from her own bed; her hair was tousled and she was wearing a very simple linen gown. "Nicias, do you wish to come with me? I will leave immediately. Every hour you are here puts you further at risk."

"I am not going to let my son leave with a perfect stranger," my mother interrupted.

Lily turned to say, "This is not your decision to make." She took a deep breath. When she spoke again, her voice reminded me of the black ice from my dream. "I lost my mother to *Ecl* before I was old enough to know her, and my twin brother several years ago. I have seen too many loved ones fall. I will not lose someone whom I have the power to save." More gently, she added, "Nicias will be safe on the island. He is of our blood, and has our magic; that means he will be allowed to study. I do not know what crimes led to your exile, but they don't matter. The Empress's laws do not allow any falcon to be held to the crimes of his parents." She sighed. "Have faith in your son. Recall that you are the ones who taught him about duty."

Turning from my mother, she touched my hand and said, "If you want to come with me, get dressed. I will go to my home and do the same, and then meet you here."

I did not need to tell her or my parents that I would be leaving for Ahnmik that morning. The decision was already made, and we all knew it.

"Wait," I said as one complication occurred to me. "I need to speak to Oliza."

"Of course," Lily said. "You are sworn to her. I will meet you outside the nest, then."

She kissed me on the cheek before pushing past my parents on her way out.

My mother sighed, her head bowed in defeat. She touched my cheek, almost whispering, "She's right, Nicias. It's fools' hopes that make us want to keep you here."

"May I speak to Nicias alone for a moment?" my father asked. My mother nodded and drifted back into the hallway without another word.

"Are you really worried that I won't return to Wyvern's Court?" I asked. "This is my home. I consider myself a subject of the Tuuli Thea and the Diente and their heir, not of some empress I have never met. And though Araceli may be family by blood, the falcons have never claimed me as kin. All the family I care about is here."

My father drew a deep breath.

"Ahnmik is, despite all its other traits, a beautiful land," he finally said. "It is a realm where you would be revered instead of shunned, where your falcon features would be seen as a thing of beauty instead of proof that you are different. That alone can be a powerful lure."

I shook my head. "Vanity isn't enough to make me betray Oliza."

"More than that, on Ahnmik you would be royalty. You would be able to use magic that few people here can even begin to comprehend." I had no desire to rule over anyone. And although I was curious about magic, I wasn't curious enough to give up everything—and everyone—for it. "And then, of course, there is—what is her name?" he asked me softly.

"Lily," I answered. "She has been my friend for two years. I know I should have told you, but . . ."

My father shook his head. "I speak to you now because I know Araceli will offer you everything and more to keep you by her side, and I hope you will have weighed all the possible temptations against your love for and duty toward this land."

I nodded, knowing what he was implying. "Before you go, there is something I need to show you, for you to remember when Araceli tells you of the wonders of the white city."

He unlaced the throat of his shirt and pulled the cloth over his head.

I knew many men in the local guard who practiced bare-chested in the summer heat, and even more who wore the low-backed shirts that allowed them to grow the wings of a Demi form at any time, but I had never seen my father dressed either way.

Now I realized why.

Complex designs had been etched into his skin; scars covered his back and crept onto his shoulders and upper arms. Some were fine and neat, as if from a sharp blade, and some were broader and appeared burned in—as if he had been branded.

I stepped forward, horrified not only by the cruelty of whoever had left these marks, but by the artistry of the marks as well. Shimmering lines of what had to be magic twined with the scars, continuing and layering the designs in iridescent silver, blue and violet.

Someone had created a work of art on my father's skin, with blades and power.

"It is a crime to imply that the royal family can be cruel, so on the island punishment is referred to as the Empress's or Heir's mercy. It equates to torture. Many things on Ahnmik are equally honey coated—especially when it comes to the royal family. Keep that in mind. Keep in mind that if you choose to stay, you will be tying yourself to leaders who condone such things."

"What did you do?" I asked in shock. I had never dared to question either of my parents about why they had been exiled from the land of their birth. But I had never seen the punishment they had received, either.

"My crime was wanting to live off the island, among those the falcons consider savages—the avians and serpiente you have been raised with. Your mother wears similar marks, though hers are worse. In addition to leaving, she argued with my mother to let me go. After Araceli decided we were no longer suited to life on Ahnmik, after she had decided to let us go, and bound our powers, it was pure spite that led her to mark us both."

Suddenly the idea of visiting the white city filled me with dread.

My father grasped my shoulders in a brief and uncharacteristic embrace. "You've falcon blood, but your heart is avian, Nicias. You'll come back to us."

✳✳✳

The dancers in the front of the nest tried to keep me from entering at first. They relented only when I pressed upon them that it was an emergency, and even then they did so reluctantly.

No, a falcon was not welcome in this place.

I found Oliza still sleeping, resting innocently in a tangle with several other dancers. I couldn't reach her past the others, so I called her name.

"Oliza?"

"Nicias?" She sat up so quickly that one of the serpents who had been lying against her whispered a sleepy complaint before another shifted to fill in the gap Oliza had left behind. "What's wrong?"

I winced, knowing that anything I said in the dancer's nest would become common knowledge within a day. The dancers were revered in serpiente society as historians and storytellers—which made them tend to be insatiable gossips.

When I hesitated to explain around company, Oliza stood and followed me to the edge of the nest. Out of earshot of the rest, I said simply, "Apparently I inherited my parents' magic. It seems to come with some disadvantages."

Oliza's eyes widened. "I hope it doesn't pose a danger."

My gut tightened. "My parents think it does. I don't understand it all, really. But I'm traveling to Ahnmik, as soon as possible." Belatedly, I added, "With your leave?"

"Permission granted, of course, especially if your safety is at stake," she answered swiftly. "We will see you again, I hope?"

"I'm one of your Wyverns," I answered without hesitation. "And I would far rather live in a realm you rule than that of the falcon Empress."

"Take care of yourself, Nicias," Oliza said, with more warmth in her voice than she ever allowed herself to show around her many suitors. She hugged me tightly and kissed my cheek. I heard one of the serpents who had been watching us say something that sounded like "Lucky falcon."

Lucky. At the moment, *lucky* was not a word I would apply to myself.

CHAPTER 4

"THE FLIGHT is long," Lily warned me, barely a single step outside the nest, "and there aren't many places to rest. We'll be able to stop and relax our wings, and perhaps eat something, only once during the journey—provided we make good enough time to get to the island at low tide, while it's above water." Her eyes widened. "Nicias . . ."

She reached forward and tugged my hair loose of the tie I used to keep it back.

"What are—"

She laughed. "I was too preoccupied in your room to notice earlier." She pulled forward some of the front strands, allowing me to see for the first time that what had previously been silver-white was now pale blue, just a shade lighter than my eyes.

Normally the change would have irritated me, since it set me even further apart from the serpents and avians who already looked at me as an oddity. However, Lily's delight was infectious.

"A falcon's magic marks his body," she explained. "Your

36

mother's violet eyes are one example. The blue in your hair is another. It will probably darken a little more when you begin to study, though the royals don't seem to show their power as overtly as some of the others. But I'm delaying us; we should be gone. Are you ready?"

"I hope so," I answered.

She didn't wait for more, shifting immediately into a sleek peregrine falcon a little smaller than me.

The first leg of the flight was less terrible than I had imagined, despite Lily's being able to hold an even faster pace than Oliza had ever managed. At the beginning, I delighted in spreading my wings, delighted in the ocean breeze and the smell of brine. I settled into a peaceful reflection, caught between sun and sea.

Then Lily bumped against me, her talons catching my wings to steady and lift me. With a start, I realized that I had dipped dangerously close to the waves. I shook my wings vigorously, both to gain altitude and to dry my feathers.

Though we had left shortly after dawn, we did not reach the island Lily had spoken of until nearly dusk. The little bit of volcanic rock, worn smooth and covered with shelled creatures and seaweed, was an inhospitable place to rest, but I was still grateful for the chance to return to human form for a while.

I arched my back, stretching my spine and then rolling my shoulders, unable to focus on fears or hopes while my heartbeat was still pounding from the exertion of the day.

As she landed, Lily shed the last of her illusions, then for the first time stood before me in her natural form. She ducked her head self-consciously as I stared, shocked by the transformation.

Her face and form were very similar to before, but her

skin had paled to cream. Her hair was a shade darker than mine, but still the color of honey in milk; in the front, it became cobalt and indigo, like gemstones spun into silk. Her eyes, previously a very ordinary blue-gray, now picked up the colors of the ocean and of her hair, so that they too shone like fair jewels.

And she was wearing her wings, enormous peregrine wings that tumbled down from her shoulders and nearly brushed the ground at her feet.

"I know it is rare in Wyvern's Court for one to wear her wings openly," she said shyly, "but on Ahnmik, very few do not. This is what I consider my true form."

She knelt and brushed a hand over the kelp that covered the island, clearing a bare, smooth space large enough for both of us to sit in.

"I hope I didn't overstep my bounds with your parents earlier," she said. "This must be very hard for them. They both left Ahnmik when they were young, and having their magic bound would have been terribly painful. It is not surprising that they would not think well of the royal house."

"How could they?" I almost asked, thinking of my father's scars. But I kept my questions to myself when I saw the fear in her eyes. "I saw them hesitate, and all I could think was that they couldn't possibly know . . . They hadn't felt your heartbeat slow and your skin cool as your magic tried to drag you down. I shouldn't have taken my fear out on them." I reached out, and she took my hand. "You're safe now. And you probably have questions."

Questions. Where could I begin? "Until last night, my parents had always refused to speak of Ahnmik—or magic."

My parents had tried to forget their pasts, and who they used to be. My father had changed his name entirely, from

Sebastian to Andreios, which he had been known by for all the years he had hidden among the avians as a crow. Both of my parents had chosen to use the surname Silvermead after their exile, in honor of the avian family that had taken my mother in when she had first fled the island, and of the dancer Valene, who had petitioned the Empress for their pardon.

"What would you like to know?" Lily asked, startling me from my thoughts. I had to stop drifting off. Of course, that was exactly what this trip was about, wasn't it?

"That moment in the woods—the one that made you so sure I had this magic—can you explain it to me?"

How could I possess something I barely understood?

"When a falcon's magic first appears, it often does unpredictable things," she said. I could see her struggling to find the right words for something that was common knowledge among her people. "The three visions might have been images from your future, necessary sights, catalysts with the power to irrevocably alter your path." Then she added with a wry smile, "Or they might have been nothing more than ghosts, people you might see, or even ones who sensed the sudden shift in magic and happened to look back at you. Blue and even silver eyes are so common on Ahnmik that I couldn't begin to guess to whom they might belong. And cobra eyes are certainly not unlikely in your future." She dismissed it all with a shake of her head. "I won't go so far as to say that all visions are without meaning, but those that come unsummoned to an undisciplined mind are most often nonsense."

"Is there anything you think that I should know, before we get to Ahnmik?"

Lily paused, fiddling with a razor-shell she had taken from the rocks. "The island may seem very overpowering when you first land. People will be able to tell that you are royal blood, and they may not know how to treat you. The royal court of Ahnmik is not as informal as the one you are used to, and people are likely to err on the side of caution.

"Araceli will probably give you leave to address her familiarly, but usually any member of the royal house is addressed as lady or, in Servos's case, as sir." Slanting an amused gaze in my direction, she added, "I suppose that means I have been horribly disrespectful with you these two years, calling you Nicias."

The suggestion made me laugh and shake my head. I was the son of two guards, and only a guard myself, which placed me one respectful step *below* the lords and ladies of Wyvern's Court. I couldn't imagine being treated as some kind of royalty on Ahnmik.

"Aside from you, the royal house has four members. Cjarsa is Empress, but she rarely grants audiences, and it is Araceli who rules the island day to day. Syfka is right hand to both Cjarsa and Araceli, and often speaks for them when they are otherwise occupied. She is also the one who normally sees to any business off the island." Syfka was rarely spoken of in Wyvern's Court, though I recognized her name from my parents' conversations. I understood that she had enabled my father to leave Ahnmik the first time and helped my mother and father both return from the island after Araceli had taken them. If Araceli proved herself as malicious as my father had painted her, then perhaps I would find an ally in Syfka. "Servos, the last of the four, is guardian to the *shm'Ecl*."

As my parents had, she spoke the word softly, her gaze haunted.

"You should recall that we falcons share history with the serpiente, not the avians," she continued. "If I had considered

40

more carefully, I would have disguised myself as a serpent instead of an avian in Wyvern's Court, so I would not need to deal with men who felt like they had to protect the honor of a woman living alone and were shocked if I displayed an unseemly emotion." She shrugged, but I understood her point. Only the serpiente influence in Wyvern's Court had given her the freedom to maintain her independence while utilizing such a disguise. "You'll find that most falcons are as free with their emotions as the serpiente.

"Hmm, what else?" she asked, pondering. I saw her gaze at the edge of the island, which had already lost several inches to the rising tide. It would not be long before our dry resting place became ocean once again. "Of course, the old language is spoken on Ahnmik. You've been studying it in your history lessons at Wyvern's Court, but it might take you a little while to perfect its use."

Not too long, I hoped.

"Ahnmik is in your blood," Lily added, as if she could read my mind. "His words will feel natural to you."

She leaned on me, her body warm against mine. "It is a beautiful land, Nicias. Though I have enjoyed seeing other places these last two years, I have missed the white city. I have missed hearing her sing, and seeing the magic dance, and being among others who see my blue and know what it means instead of simply fearing it. You will see. Wyvern's Court is a lovely place . . . but it is not Ahnmik."

CHAPTER 5

W E SHIFTED INTO our human forms just above the
ground and landed on a marble terrace. My knees almost went out from under me, I was so exhausted. We had
flown throughout the night, and it was now well past sunup
once again.

I was barely aware of the audience we had attracted, until
someone spoke to me.

Even once I had lifted my head to listen to his words, I
had no idea what he was saying. If I had been less exhausted, I
probably could have translated the old language, but right
then my mind refused to obey.

I blinked at him for a moment, trying to figure out what
was going on.

Thankfully Lily noticed my confusion. "He wishes to
know if you need anything," she told me.

I knew what I needed: sleep. I was having trouble standing upright; I felt as if I was being buffeted by winds from all
directions, and my vision was blurry from exhaustion.

I should greet the Empress first, I thought. *Or—*

Lily stepped forward to answer for me. Her voice rang with authority, the rolling language of Ahnmik coming easily to her despite the two years she had spent in Wyvern's Court. After a moment, she turned back to me and added, "They will find you somewhere to rest, and something to eat if you wish it. I apologize, but I must leave you in the capable hands of our welcoming committee, so I can present myself to my lady and let her know I am ready to return to my duties. Get some sleep."

"I can help you to your rooms, sir," a young man offered, making an effort to speak a language I knew.

As tired as I was, I did not fail to notice that the rooms I was given were more elegant than the ones Oliza occupied back in Wyvern's Court. If the pale stone and crystal sculpture lacked some of the warmth of that place, they made up for it with sparkling beauty.

My guide left me in the hands of two women, each wearing loose slacks and backless shirts, and each graced with wings that matched my own peregrine. Everyone I had seen so far had worn Demi wings, as Lily had said.

And everyone, in either the language I knew or the language I could barely understand, seemed to want to know what I needed. While I fought to stay awake, being waited on was fine with me. I wouldn't be able to exert any kind of effort if I tried.

The meal I was served was simple but delicious: freshly baked bread still hot from the oven, a savory fish soup that warmed me to the core and hot cider to drink.

As I ate, I was entertained by a choir somewhere outside the building. The words faded in and out of my awareness, but the melody was haunting.

Food and a moment to regain my bearings had helped

enough that when I was asked, "Would you like a bath read-ied, sir?" I had the sense to answer, "My name is Nicias."

The woman nodded. "Yes, sir."

Being called sir again sent a chill down my spine. "You can call me Nicias."

Her eyes widened a little, but she repeated, "Nicias. Would you like—"

"I think I'd rather sleep first, if you don't mind."

"Of course," she answered. "You have been shown your room?"

"Yes, I'm fine. . . . Please, I'd just like to sleep now."

Within two breaths I was left alone to seek my bed, accompanied only by the distant singing.

The bed was larger than I was used to, as everything here seemed to be, but firm enough to be comfortable and piled with the softest blankets I had ever touched.

Only as I was looking for a lamp or candle to snuff out did I realize that the abundant light seemed to be coming from the walls themselves. More specifically, from intricate designs etched into the stone.

If I knew how to use falcon magic, I would probably be able to turn them off, I thought, with as much humor as I could muster.

For now, I would have to be content with light. But the instant I lay down and got settled, the lights dimmed and finally shut off. The effect startled me so much that I stood up, prompting them to gradually brighten until I lay down again.

The colors in my dreams seemed brighter than usual, and the sounds softer. A melody wove itself through everything, sometimes sounding like a chorus of hundreds singing in harmony all around me, and sometimes sounding like a lone child far away. No matter how I tried, I couldn't quite make out the words.

Visions came and disappeared throughout the night.

A woman was kneeling on a floor of pure white stone with her head bent forward. Her hair was so white it seemed almost translucent, except at the front, where it darkened to violet and, finally, almost black; it fell forward, hiding her face and pooling on the floor around her. Silks that shimmered from deep indigo to silver wrapped her form in a complex gown.

Suddenly I realized that those silks not only clothed her, but bound her. Her wrists were crossed behind her back and tied there. Her eyes were covered and her ankles were pressed together.

Despite the blindfold, she looked up as I approached.

"Hehj-ale'heah-gen'lo'Mehay?" the wind seemed to whisper.

I found that I understood her words easily: Do you desire to know your future?

"No," I answered.

She gave a tight-lipped smile. "No man, no woman, can see the future in truth. It is all the same illusion. *Hehj-ale'heah-gen'lo'Ecl?"* Do you desire to know your past?

"No," I answered again.

"We will be here before," she said.

"I don't understand."

"You didn't," she answered. "Now you do." She began to sing, a melody slightly different than the ones I had heard earlier. It made the air ripple around us.

Then the world changed, and we were standing on the cold black ice I knew from my nightmares, with the bone white moon above. The woman's gyrfalcon wings were spread, her hair whipping around her in a wind so strong, I stumbled and tore the skin of my hands on the sharp ice. The silks that had bound her were gone, and now she was wearing a gown that looked to be made of woven gold.

Her song had changed into a scream, one that made the ice shudder around us. "This isn't your place, Nicias," she shrieked, voice like the wind. "Leave now. Dance with the light, falcon child."

I was thrown from my dream with the force of a thunderbolt and woke breathless. I flung myself out of bed and was grateful when the light snapped on. The door to the next room had been left partially open, revealing a bath that had been prepared recently enough that the water was still perfectly warm. Or perhaps magic had kept it that way for hours. I didn't know or care.

I scrubbed my skin and hair, dried with a soft towel and dressed in clothing that had been hung while I had slept.

The pants were made of a material that was softer and warmer than any I was familiar with; in lieu of a belt, they had a silver clasp on each side. The legs were comfortable and unrestricting, but laced tightly at the calves. The shirt was similar, designed to be loose around the shoulders and in the upper sleeves, but tight at the forearms and wrists. The upper back was open to allow for wings. There was no footwear, but thinking back, I didn't recall seeing any of the falcons wearing shoes the day before.

I had just finished tying back my hair when the first knock came on my door.

"Yes?"

The young woman who entered was the one I had instructed to call me Nicias the evening before. She curtsied deeply, bowing her head.

I stared at her for too long, waiting for her to rise, before it occurred to me to say, "Stand up. Can I help you?"

She stood with a smile, as if she could have knelt on my

floor all day. "I hope the room merited your approval, and you found everything you needed this morning?"

Even if something had bothered me, I wouldn't have dared to say no—not to someone who was trying so hard to please me. "Everything was fine."

"The Heir would like to see you this morning," she said, "as soon as you are ready."

Before I could say that I was ready, she reached forward to change how the cuff of my shirt was laced.

I pulled back so quickly that she dropped her gaze apologetically. "Please, my lady will be very cross with me if I let you go about Ahnmik and the palace looking like a mongrel. You don't know our ways yet. Let me help?"

Despite the sincerity in her voice, I did not care for the term "mongrel." I lived in a mixed-blood land. Moreover, I knew that the word's equivalent in the old language, *quemak*, was considered by the serpiente to be uncivil. A fight would have broken out in Wyvern's Nest if one of the serpiente dancers had used it as casually as this woman just had.

She must have seen my displeasure; I saw her pale ever so slightly. I recalled my father's warning about the Empress's "mercy" and realized exactly why she was so desperate to please me—and Araceli.

I bit my tongue. I didn't want to be responsible for getting this girl—or myself—into trouble.

"I would appreciate your help," I said finally. "But please teach me so I can do it right on my own in the future."

She clapped her hands lightly, a gesture of relief and joy. "Of course!"

Over the next few minutes, I learned one crucial thing: Falcons valued appearance far too much. I had always cared somewhat about how I looked, but that was mostly out of respect for Oliza. As one of her guards, I reflected upon her.

I would try to extend that respect toward the Empress and her heir, but I couldn't help complaining when my tutor took down my hair so that she could clasp most of the blond bulk back while leaving the newly blue strands loose around my face.

"A falcon's blue is a thing to be very proud of," she explained when I reached forward to tuck those irritating strands back, "not something to be hidden."

I didn't have the heart to contradict her. I was beginning to look forward to meeting Araceli for only one reason: I wanted to have my powers bound, so that I could get off this island and go back to being Nicias Silvermead, Wyvern of Honor, instead of some preened and pampered prince of an empire ruled by fear.

Finally she asked me to grow the wings of my Demi form. "People will be very confused if they see you without them. They will wonder what you and the Lady could possibly have fought about this soon."

"Fought?" I inquired.

"Those who are a danger to the city or endangered by the city are not allowed to spread wing above her, or wear their Demi forms. That includes criminals, Pure Diamond, outsiders, and mongrels. But you are pure royal blood; the only reason you would be denied access to our sky is if the Empress or her heir barred you from it."

I frowned at the way she separated the classes of the city so easily.

"They're restricted for different reasons, of course," she added, apologetically. "Pure Diamond is a rank for falcons who learn their magic too young. They are often . . . disturbed, and need to be bound as children to keep them from harming themselves or others. Empress Cjarsa prefers that they stay on land, so that it is easier to reach them if they need her.

"As for outsiders, they are kept grounded mostly for their own protection. The city is not kind to those it does not consider its own, and it can be very disorienting from above.

"As for those with mixed blood . . ." She hesitated, and I wondered if she had intentionally changed her phrasing due to my response to the word *mongrel*. "They often have trouble controlling their magic. It makes them dangerous to others, and to themselves. They must stay on the ground, where the city's power protects them somewhat."

And what would Araceli think of me? I wondered. Despite this girl's assurance that I was royal blood, I was most certainly an outsider. I was sworn to a mixed-blood queen and I was the son of two of Ahnmik's exiled criminals. How long would it be before I was thrown into one of those sharply defined categories?

CHAPTER 6

BEFORE I COULD LEAVE my room, I had to have my hair put up, my clothing corrected and my feathers carefully preened. If this was a taste of royalty, I would have no difficulty refusing any offer Araceli might make. This much attention was more than I'd ever wanted, and stepping into the open streets was a blessed relief.

In the first breathtaking moment, I realized how little of Ahnmik I had seen the day before.

The road, the walls, every building about me glistened with the same kinds of designs as were in my room; only here, instead of simply remaining silver, the patterns shifted from sea foam and emerald to coral pink and bruised cranberry. The designs seemed to dance to the music that I suddenly realized was coming not from a chorus, but from the walls.

Magic.

The road beneath my bare feet was warm, and though it looked as hard as crystal, when I stepped down, it felt as soft as a carpet.

"What are the towers ahead of us?" I asked, pointing to three pure white spires in the north.

"*Yenna'marl,*" my guide answered. "They are called simply the white towers, and they mark the boundaries of the testing yard. The rest of the city holds spells to keep her inhabitants' magic in check so that they can learn faster than their power can grow. But in that yard, the magic is even stronger than it is in the outside world. Careful not to stray there; the way the magic flares can be dangerous, until you have more control."

I nodded, appreciating the advice.

We had reached the arched doorway of a grand building that seemed to be made entirely of crystal, perfectly clear save what must have been hundreds of layers of magic.

We paused at the doorway, and I tried to follow the patterns as they wove under and over each other.

Suddenly it seemed so obvious. "It's writing, isn't it?" I asked in surprise. "What does this say?"

My guide looked startled. "It's not writing in the sense that you know."

"But . . . here," I argued, tracing one line. I couldn't make my eyes follow it exactly, but I still understood. "It's a prayer."

"We should go inside," she said.

"One moment, please." I struggled to grasp what I was "reading." The longer I watched the pattern, the more loudly it seemed to speak to me.

A prayer to Ahnmik.

Then the voice from my dream the night before whispered, *Nicias, child of she who is heir to the domain of ice and night, you sing here so clearly. So, careful, Nicias, remember.*

We will be here before.

"Nicias!"

I was wrenched back by the shoulders, spun around so quickly that I felt dizzy and reached out a hand to support myself.

Someone grabbed my wrist, steadying me as I blinked away my confusion.

"Vesake-mana," my guide was mumbling from where she knelt beside us.

"Ka'gen'lakin," the woman who had caught me replied.

It took me a moment to translate the brief exchange—*I'm sorry, Lady. Not your fault*—and meanwhile the woman caught my arm. *"Sine'le,"* she said, dismissing my guide, before addressing me. "Nicias, come inside."

I did as instructed, my throat parched and my eyes unfocused. "Careful, Nicias, or we'll lose you to the *shm'Ecl* before the day is out. Do you know *nothing* of your magic? Did your father . . . Of course not." She sighed. She pressed a cup into my hands and said, "Drink."

The liquid burned my tongue as I gulped it down too quickly, but it also managed to clear my head.

Suddenly I realized that my guide had addressed this woman as Lady; she was either the Empress or her heir, then. My gaze snapped up, and instantly I knew which one.

Those eyes. I knew them from that moment in the woods; when my magic had first appeared, it was her gaze that had first looked upon me.

Furthermore, these were the ice blue eyes that looked back at me from the mirror every day. Softened in some places and sharpened in others, her face was nearly the female version of my own. She smiled as I looked at her, scanning my features as I did hers.

"Son of my son," she greeted me. "Nicias of Ahnmik."

"Silvermead," I corrected automatically before it occurred to me that I might offend her.

She shook her head, laughing a little. "Your mother might have taken the name Silvermead, but your father was my son. You have the powerful wings of a peregrine, as he did, and as I do. If you did not have our magic, the songs would not call to you the way they do. Ever since I felt your magic wake a few days ago, I have known that you are worthy of your royal blood. On this island, that makes you Nicias of Ahnmik, nothing less."

I wanted to ask what she'd meant when she'd said she had felt my magic wake, why I had seen her so briefly, and who the other eyes had belonged to, for if hers had been real, then perhaps the others had been, too.

Instead, I hardened my heart against the joy I could see in her face and forced myself to say what I needed to. "I'm sorry, Lady, but I don't want to be Nicias of Ahnmik; I want only to be Nicias Silvermead. My parents sent me here to have my powers bound, so I can safely return to Wyvern's Court."

Araceli winced. "Nicias, why? What can you have there that is more than we can give you here? You weren't raised to rule, so I can understand your being daunted by that. You weren't raised in luxury, so I can understand your not desiring the finer things Ahnmik can provide you. But what does *that* world offer you? Not even love, Nicias, unless you are willing to kill any child your mate would have."

Her voice softened as she implored, "Give this world a chance." I started to argue, but she shook her head. "Nicias, I've lived nearly two millennia, and have had only one child. Letting him leave was the most painful thing I have ever done."

"Painful for whom?" I asked, knowing that my voice was harsh, but the image of my father's scars was still bitter in my memory.

"You have no concept of what our magic can do if uncontrolled," she snapped. "Your mother might have survived, though few born with power can survive long without this land's magic to protect them. Your father certainly would not have. He didn't have the training, and royal blood cannot protect one forever. The only way I could bind their magics as tightly as I needed to was to etch the spells into their skin. Even what I did might not be enough; the marks clearly weren't as strong as they should have been, or you never would have been born with power."

She spoke with such pain in her voice, I couldn't help wondering if it was true. What if the wounds she'd dealt *had* been part of the spell to keep my parents' magic from killing them? Who was I to call her a liar, I who knew nothing about this dangerous power except that even my parents were frightened by it?

"I'm sorry, Lady," I replied, shamed by my arrogance.

She sighed. "Forgiven. And please, Nicias, to you I am Araceli."

I nodded. "Araceli. I'm sorry for my impertinence a moment ago. But I still don't think this place is right for me. As you said, I wasn't raised with luxury, or servants hovering over me and calling me sir; I don't think I would become used to it, or even want to."

Again she laughed a little, the sound like bells. "Nicias, consider for a moment. For one, you are fascinating to most of the people of Ahnmik; very rarely is one of us born off the island, much less one of royal blood. Furthermore, they didn't know how much attention you would demand. If you were spoiled and arrogant and wanted to be pampered, but they ignored you, you would be far more cross than if you were modest and kind and wanted only to be left alone while they hovered. If you let them know that you prefer to be treated like an equal, that is how they will treat you."

It was difficult to reconcile the horrible person my father and mother had warned me about with the woman I was speaking to now.

"Come walk with me, Nicias," Araceli requested. "Let me present you to Empress Cjarsa, and then I shall show you around our island. You can tell me this evening whether you want your powers bound so soon. I'll warn you now, it will hurt, and it will leave you marked, and it will be irreversible. To bind your magic, I must bind your falcon form. You'll never be able to spread wing again, Nicias. I pray you will give this world a chance before you decide to throw it all away."

We walked through the palace, but its wonder was lost on me.

Pain I could deal with, if I had to. My training in Oliza's guard had taught me how to brace myself against necessary pain. Marks I could deal with. My falcon blood had already marked me, setting me apart from the others at Wyvern's Court both physically and mentally. I could stand losing magic I had never expected, and a royal position I had never wanted, too.

But never to fly again?

Never to set off into the sky I loved, alone or with Oliza? Never to return to the distant lands that could be reached only by wing?

I wouldn't lose just the air. I would lose Wyvern's Court. With none of the strengths of a falcon, a serpent or an avian, I would have nothing to offer as Oliza's guard. They might let me stay out of pity, but living the rest of my life in the face of that pity would destroy me.

Yet both of my parents had avian forms, even though their magic had been bound.... "How did my parents get their winged forms?"

Araceli winced as she answered, "Force-change. It is one of the higher-level abilities, and forbidden on the island in all but the most desperate situations. It is a way to temporarily take control of another's magic and body. Afterward, a skilled user of our magic retains a memory of the forms of the person he changed."

"Why is it forbidden?"

Araceli looked at me as if I was mad. "To violate another's body, magic and mind so intimately is . . ." She shook her head. "Among my people, force-change is seen in the same light as the serpents you were raised among see rape."

"If it is so abhorrent," I said tightly, "then why was it taught to both of my parents?"

"Kel was taught to force-change because she was one of the Empress's personal guards, and although the Mercy almost never need to utilize such a skill, a guardian of the royal house must be armed with as much knowledge as she can have. Sebastian . . ." Her voice wavered as she said my father's falcon name. "He was royal blood, as you are. I had no need to teach him any specific pattern; he could discover it on his own, as in time you probably will be able to, too. If you decide not to go through with this self-destructive binding, I will teach you the discipline you need to keep your magic from harming you. The rest, for royal blood, comes naturally."

"I still have trouble imagining my parents doing something they were raised to feel was so evil."

Araceli backtracked gracefully, but the distaste was not completely gone from her voice as she added, "I am sure your parents did it out of desperation. I understand both of them were attempting to save another's life. Even in this city, they would not have been reprimanded for that effort."

I wanted to ask more about that story, but Araceli's tone made it clear that the discussion was over. We walked silently for a minute and soon approached a pair of doors, each pale blue with a pattern like silver frost on the glass. A falcon guard stood on each side of them, watching us warily.

"Please tell Cjarsa that I would like to introduce her to Sebastian's son," Araceli told the guards.

"I regret to inform you that the Lady is not receiving today," one answered. Both dropped their gazes as Araceli frowned.

"I'm not some mongrel seeking to petition for a favor," she said coolly.

The door opened, and out stepped a falcon I recognized from history-book sketches: Syfka. She bowed respectfully to Araceli, but her voice held poorly concealed annoyance as she explained, "You won't be able to speak to her. I've already pushed my way past these guards; the Lady is occupied, with no time for conversation." Under her breath, she grumbled, "As she has been for weeks."

Araceli sighed and glanced at me apologetically. "Nicias, allow me to present Syfka, aplomado of the royal house and our ambassador on the mainland. Syfka, this is Nicias, son of Kel and Sebastian."

Syfka's gaze fell on me, and I saw a hint of regret in her eyes as she greeted me politely. "An honor to be introduced, sir." Before I could reply, she turned back to Araceli. "My lady, might I have a few moments of your time?"

"Can it wait? I would rather not leave Nicias alone on his first day in our city."

"As you wish, but it is a matter of some importance to both of us. I had wished to take it up with Cjarsa directly . . ." She shrugged. "It seems the Lady has more pressing concerns than her own kingdom." Araceli looked at Syfka sharply, and the aplomado quickly assured her, "No disrespect intended. As for Nicias, he is blood of our house; the land and his people will protect him, if he needs it. Ahnmik would never betray its prince, so he is in no danger wandering alone. And perhaps he would appreciate a few minutes unchaperoned, to think."

Seeing my dismissal very near, I interjected, "If I might ask one favor?"

"Yes?" Araceli replied.

"Before I make my decision on whether to stay or go, I would like to speak to my parents." They had warned me not to trust this woman. I didn't know whether she was speaking the truth about my magic and my falcon form.

"Nicias, Nicias." Araceli sighed. "When you leave this island, it must be with your magic either bound or mastered. Right now, the island is protecting you from yourself, and yet you were still hypnotized by your power at the doorway to the palace. If you try to leave now, you'll fall and drown while you're busy listening to *Ecl*'s whispers and watching the paintings in the waves."

I recalled the way Lily had needed to grab my wings so I wouldn't fall on my way to the island. I didn't think I could risk a return trip. "Then might one of them come here?"

"Your parents are both in exile," Araceli told me bluntly.

"But you are the heir to the Empress. You must have the authority to lift that sentence long enough for them to speak to me. If you have been honest so far, then there is no risk to you in my speaking to them."

Syfka took a step back as I made that statement, even before Araceli tensed, looking as offended as if I had struck her.

"I do *not* have that authority. That is my lady Cjarsa's decision to make, as she is the one who put down the sentence upon each of them. Even if it *was* my decision," she continued, "I would not allow them back. When they fled this island, they endangered themselves, and they endangered those they'd sworn their loyalty to on the mainland.

"Your mother fled her responsibility to the Empress Cjarsa the first time she was called upon to protect her liege. Tell me, Nicias, what is the sentence among Oliza's Wyverns for a guard who abandons his post and allows his monarch to face an assassin alone?"

She did not wait for me to unravel my tongue and attempt to answer. Among the serpiente and the avians, what she was describing would be high treason, and punishable by death.

"In the years since they left," she said more softly, "it seems that both of your parents have matured. Their positions among the avians are respected, and their loyalty is unquestioned. Perhaps they have learned their lesson. But that does not excuse their first crimes. They abandoned this land when it needed them. If you stay as prince, you might have the power to pardon them someday, but until then I will not allow either one to set foot in my city."

"And what unforgivable crime did your son commit?" I asked tentatively.

Araceli's tone when she spoke of my father was like ice.

"Sebastian of Ahnmik is dead. There is a crow who holds his memories, a crow who holds his blood but not his features—the features I see so clearly in you. But my son, my only son, is dead to this world, dead to my people, and dead to me."

"What—"

"Silence," she snapped, and now the pain in her eyes was apparent. "On this topic, I demand it. We do not speak of that which is too late to change."

"My lady, I hate to interrupt," Syfka said softly, stepping forward awkwardly, "but I must speak with you, *now*."

Araceli nodded. "Walk our city if you like, Nicias," she said, distantly. "I have business I must attend to. I will summon you this evening to hear your decision. Dismissed."

I took a step away from the pair, somewhat dazed by the argument. When I had just turned the first corner, I heard Araceli say to Syfka, "I suppose it is too much to ask for his trust, when his parents have surely been speaking ill of me throughout his life. Even though I speak honestly to him and say things he would accept as reasonable if they came from a serpent or an avian, he assumes they are lies."

"Doubtless his parents think many of their words are deserved," Syfka answered.

I hesitated, curious what else they would say when they thought I was not listening.

"Perhaps some of them are," Araceli admitted. "But our war with the serpiente was over thousands of years ago, and yet they still teach their children a hatred of us." After a long silence, during which I almost continued on my way, she added, "I cannot stand to lose another child to ancient conflicts, Syfka. But how can I compete with a hatred that has endured thousands of years?"

The raw pain in Araceli's voice cut me more deeply than anything she had said so far.

As a child of Wyvern's Court, I was far too familiar with her sentiment. I had seen serpents wary of avians, and avians wary of serpents, despite the efforts our leaders had made to bring the two groups together. I had thought myself beyond that hatred because I had been born a falcon. Instead, I had learned to hate my own blood.

I continued on my way out, tracing the halls I had come through with Araceli, and resolved to try to look upon what I found here with a more open mind. I would not dismiss everything my parents had told me, but I would try not to be as biased as an avian matron watching the serpents' dance.

CHAPTER 7

ONCE BACK OUTSIDE, I hesitated at the foot of the palace. I might have dreamed of the chance to explore this city, but to stand at its edge with no destination and no guide was overwhelming.

In the distance, I caught a glimpse of an elegant spire shimmering like a violet mirage on the horizon.

Thinking that landmark as good a destination as any, I started forward, only to find that the roads of Ahnmik twisted in unpredictable ways. What had seemed to be a straight path only moments before turned out to curve so that after several minutes I found myself on the cliffs where the ocean met the island.

Turning back, I could see the city: the three *yenna'marl*, bone white and sharp against the sky, and a trio of arches that seemed to be in the center of the city. Again, I could see only the edge of the strange violet spire.

I tried following the beach and found myself by a bridge that seemed to connect Ahnmik to another, smaller island, one peppered with lush greenery.

Exploring that area would have to wait. I had a feeling I was lost enough as it was. I glanced behind me, wanting to confirm that I could still see the *yenna'marl* and get my bearings from them.

The odd tower that had caught my attention was practically brushing against the road on which I now stood. How could that be?

It seemed almost as if the walls were made of liquid, and the violet that had seemed so bold at a distance was muted up close. The arched doors were smoke black glass, slick and ominous in the white city. They had no handles, though I could see the seam between the two. Two symbols marked that doorway: *shm'Ecl*.

If you can't, it will destroy you, my father had warned me. *It will numb your body and mind, until it drives you into what is called* shm'Ecl. *There are rooms on Ahnmik filled with those who have succumbed to it, those who could not learn to control their power. They are neither alive nor dead, neither awake nor asleep.*

I pushed against the doors almost in a daze, bracing myself for whatever lay beyond and yet needing to see the fate my parents feared so much.

Inside, the building was completely silent. All day I had been listening to the songs Ahnmik sang, music that seemed to seep from the walls and roads, but now I felt as if I had been struck deaf. The air was heavy, so thick with power that walking was like trying to move underwater.

The hall in which I stood was round, with a silver domed ceiling, and walls that were pale at the top but darkened to nearly black where they touched the floor. A spiral ramp circled along the edges of the room, ascending to where it hid the rest of the ceiling from my view and descending beneath the level of the floor. All along the walls were doorways, some open and some closed.

"*Maenka'Mehay-hena'hehj? Meanka'las?*" a deep voice asked. What lies beyond *Mehay*? Beyond eternity? The old language came more easily to me now, and I understood what he said as he continued. "Nothingness, *Ecl*. That which never was and never can be. Commonly, it is translated as destruction, but more accurately it is lack of existence."

I turned to find a man whose body and face made him appear a few years younger than I, but whose eyes, liquid blue like the ocean, gave him away as being ancient.

"The minds of the *shm'Ecl* are lost somewhere that we in this world can never hope to reach. Their magic is unpredictable. In some moments, they lash out at hallucinations, nightmares, pain that drives them ever further from us. But most times, they are simply still, their minds as numb and empty as the womb of the void."

"Servos?" I asked when he paused and stared into the distance.

He nodded, not seeming to focus entirely on me. "And you are Nicias."

Nicias?

A voice whispered through my mind, making me jump. It was one that I had heard several days before, when I had first fallen in the woods, and then again in my dreams.

Servos sighed.

I heard the song from my dream, heard it and for the first time understood the words.

Of eternity, of silence, of coldness, of stillness. Of Ecl. *He who dwells with* Ecl *knows of void. He who dwells with* Ecl *knows of death. But he who dances with* Ecl, *he is lost, for he who dances with* Ecl *brings to life the world of death. So dance.*

The song sent a shudder down my spine.

"You hear it?" Servos asked.

I nodded, searching the room for the singer.

"You can't see her from here; her room is near the top of this hall," Servos explained. "Her name was Darien. She was a dancer, and part of the highest choir. Most people cannot hear her voice, even when they stand beside her."

Of eternity, of madness, of heat, of movement. Of Mehay. *He who dwells with* Mehay *knows too much. He who dwells with* Mehay *knows of creation. But he who dances with* Mehay, *he is lost, for he who dances with* Mehay *cannot leave the dance and will face the fire. So dance.*

"If you'll excuse me," Servos said abruptly, "I need to see to one of my charges."

He did not wait for a response from me, but turned to descend the ramp underground.

Darien's song stopped and was replaced by a whispered chant:

Nicias Silvermead, Wyvern of Honor, Nicias of Ahnmik, heir to the heir of she who shines in darkness, Nicias fool child, Nicias wise one.

The words fluttered in my ears, almost teasing, sighing along a few notes from on high. Irresistibly drawn, I started up the ramp. I thought that the *shm'Ecl* were not aware of their surroundings, yet this woman who was supposedly one of them called me by my name and by many titles, some of which I used for myself and some of which I wanted no claim to.

My gaze was drawn to one of the open doorways I passed. Inside, a figure was lying on the floor, her ink-dark falcon wings crumpled behind her, broken and scored by tarlike bands of black and crimson. Unlike the graceful, delicate designs that painted the white city, these marks were vicious and ugly, but they shone with the iridescent sheen I had come to associate with falcon magic.

I did not know her by name, but I recognized the familiar line of her jaw, texture of her ebony hair and warmth of her fair skin. I was sworn to the royals of Wyvern's Court, which included the Cobriana, and I could not fail to note that this young woman had cobra blood.

I knelt and put a hand on her arm, needing to try even though I had little hope of stirring her.

Without warning, I found myself back in my nightmares. The black ice rippled and warped, jutting skyward to form razor blade walls, uneven and mazelike. Beneath it, I saw shadows moving, talons and fangs scraping the ice as they reached for me, and I shuddered.

I leapt aside as a serpent reared its head, blocking my path, the tips of its milky fangs glistening with drops of venom. As I stumbled, my arm brushed against one of the jagged walls of ice, and I gasped in pain as my skin was sliced open.

It is only illusion, I told myself, hoping that was true.

I stepped toward the serpent. There were glints of red in its eyes, like the vermilion magic on the girls' black feathers.

It spread its hood, but there was no crest on its back as I was used to from my dealings with other cobras. Only this slick black on black.

I see you've met my daughter, Hai. Darien's voice whispered through the land. *Her father was . . .* The cobra slid soundlessly into the ice, and the jagged landscape smoothed as Darien trailed off, leaving a lingering sense of sorrow.

Your mother could walk the minds of those no one else could touch, Darien told me. *It seems you have inherited her skill. I don't recommend it, not here in the Halls of shm'Ecl. The minds of Ecl's lovers are unfriendly places.*

Come to me. We need to speak.

She pushed me from the illusion.

The first thing I realized when I returned to reality was that my arm truly was cut. The cloth of my shirt was not torn, but the skin beneath was; my own blood had darkened the fabric. A black coil of magic, like that which wrapped Hai's wings, had twined around my hand, and I could feel where it snaked up my arm and across my shoulder. Cold seeped from the tarlike bands.

I stood unsteadily, holding my hand against my chest and wondering whether Servos would be able to explain all this to me. Or maybe Darien herself.

A few wobbly steps up the ramp took me to another doorway, and beyond this one, I heard a voice I knew.

"My lady suggested that I visit you this morning, to make sure I am ready to return to her side. I had a dream last night, you see," Lily was saying to a still form before her, "in which you woke. You came back to me. . . ." She sighed. "This morning when I first opened my eyes, I thought for a moment that it was true. We—"

She tensed and without turning said, "Nicias, meet my brother, Mer." Lily pushed herself to her feet, so I could see her brother clearly.

Mer's features would have given away their relationship even if Lily had not spoken of it. He knelt on the floor, his wings tucked behind him, his head bowed and his hands on his knees.

The posture was so relaxed and peaceful, he looked as if he was about to draw a breath and stand.

"Oh dear," Lily whispered as she took in my condition and swiftly crossed the room to take my hand. "Someone should have warned you. The *shm'Ecl* who respond to nothing else can sometimes still sense royal blood. Not all of them are happy to be drawn from their dreams. Hold on a moment, and I can fix this."

As she spoke, she unlaced the cuff of my sleeve and pushed the material off my arm to assess the damage. The bleeding had already stopped, and now the black lines on my skin began to fade away. Even the bloodstains on my shirt disappeared.

"Who was it?" she asked.

"A girl, further down. She looked like she had cobra blood."

"Hai," Lily said softly. "Her father was a serpent who came to this land several years ago; her mother—" She shook her head. "The Empress's laws forbid our kind from having children with outsiders, because they always turn out this way. Their magic grows too quickly, too wildly. As a young child, Hai would become lost in illusions no one else could see. One day she stopped speaking. Finally, a few years ago, she fell while dancing. She lost control of her magic, and you can see what it did to her. Even if she regains her mind, her wings are broken; she will never fly again."

"With all the magic on this island, there is no one who can heal her?" I asked.

"Hai is . . ." Lily hesitated, seeming to look for words that wouldn't offend me. "It may sound harsh, but she *is* mixed-blood. The cobra blood in her is like a poison. It will always burn her, and it will burn anyone who tries to save her. Those few who are strong enough to mindwalk the *shm'Ecl* are needed elsewhere. They cannot afford to risk themselves trying to save one *pt'vem* dancer."

She might be "one *pt'vem* dancer" on Ahnmik, but all I

could see were her torn wings and tortured body, and the pain she must be in.

Walking out of those halls with Lily, while leaving that broken cobra behind, went against every vow I had ever taken as a Wyvern of Honor, but I had to do it. There was no way to help her.

CHAPTER 8

AFTER WE LEFT the hall, we did not speak of Hai, and for some reason I felt oddly reluctant to speak of Darien.

"Are the roads really singing?" I asked instead. I had heard my parents and Lily say that they did, but I had always assumed that the phrase was a metaphor for beauty.

Only when Lily looked at me with surprise did I realize that I had fallen into the old language without thinking. It simply felt natural to me, like something remembered instead of learned.

My own surprise made her laugh. "Ahnmik's voice is the one spoken by your magic, by your blood and your dreams," she explained in the same language. "I told you that you would learn it swiftly, once you were here." Returning to my original question, she said, "Outsiders don't hear anything, but to one who is falcon-born, they sing. They also shift position. And some say that if you close your eyes and walk blindly down them, they will lead you where you should go." Wryly, she added, "But I don't recommend it. They have a dry sense of humor, and a tendency to dump unsuspecting zealots in the water, or lead them into very awkward positions. Though there is a story of a young man who found his true love when the roads led him through the back door of her house and into her bedroom."

I laughed, my curiosity piqued. Perhaps that was why I had been unable to find the halls that had caught my eye from across the island until I had turned my attention elsewhere.

"So the roads are alive in a way?"

"They're imbued with thousands of years of magic from those who live here, soaked with their dreams and thoughts, and thus given a personality of their own. Sometimes if you sing, they will sing back to you. Or sometimes they will knock you off your feet, depending on whether you can carry a tune."

"Dangerous paths to walk."

Lily stopped, tilting her head as if she had heard something. "If you would like to begin your study, Araceli is available now."

"How . . ." I trailed off because the question seemed stupid in this realm.

Lily answered anyway, though not how I had expected. Her voice brushed across my mind, as it had at Wyvern's Court.

It is a skill you will learn swiftly, she told me. "This way," she added aloud.

How long had it been since Araceli and Syfka had left me alone in the city? I had not managed once to think about the consequences of having my magic bound. How was that possible?

I had thought us far from the *yenna'marl,* but we turned a single corner and were only a few steps from the courtyard.

There was no visible fence or wall around the testing

yard, just the abrupt change from the crystalline roads to the white sand. In the center of the triangular yard was a pool of water, its surface like glass; offset around it were three white birch trees, each reaching toward the sky like a pale hand.

Araceli was kneeling there, her fingertips trailing through the still water. When she saw us, she stood and approached.

As she crossed the shimmering sand, it held no footprints, no sign that anyone had been there only moments before.

She nodded at Lily, but spoke to me. "Nicias, I apologize for leaving you alone earlier, but my meeting with Syfka could not wait. I am glad to see that you found a capable guide in my absence. Are you ready for your first lesson?"

She said this as if we had not argued the last time we had spoken, as if we had agreed and the decision had been made.

"I have some questions first, if you don't mind," I said, though I didn't know what she could say that would make me feel more certain.

My choice was either to master my magic, or to have it bound. If I had it bound at this point, I would be giving up everything. Perhaps I could learn just enough to be able to do a force-change. I recalled the harsh way Araceli had spoken of that magic. I knew that even if I found someone willing to donate his wings, I would never be able to take them.

"Yes?" At Araceli's prompting, I struggled to put my thoughts into coherent order.

"I do still intend to go back to Wyvern's Court," I asserted.

She nodded.

"By studying here, am I tying myself to this land? Or will I be able to leave when I choose?"

"I learned from your father that one does not attempt to imprison a prince in his own kingdom," Araceli said, her words obviously chosen with care. "Once I believe you have enough control over your magic to survive off this island, I will let you leave. You are lucky in that your royal blood will *enable* you to gain that kind of control. Most falcons are never able to safely leave the island."

I heard the prerequisite in her promise. "And if I chose to leave today?"

"I wouldn't need to stop you," she said. "I would need only to send Lillian to pick you up out of the ocean, hopefully before you sank too deep for us to bring you back."

I shuddered at the unpleasant image. "Can you give me some idea of how long it will be, then, before you will deem it safe for me to leave?"

"Falcon children are tested for their magic for the first time when they are four years old. They grow up using magic; they begin to memorize its patterns as naturally as they learn to speak and walk." She paused to consider. "The bonds on your parents and the way in which you were raised denied you that early training. I don't doubt that once you gain *any* control over your power, you will learn its finer points quickly. However, I don't know how difficult that first step might be." The first hints of impatience slipping into her voice, she added, "The sooner you allow me to begin your instruction, the sooner we can find out."

She was right. I didn't really have a choice, except for whether to keep fighting the inevitable.

I had one more question, though, about a term I had heard recently. "What is mindwalking?"

Araceli looked startled. She looked at Lily, who said, "I

mentioned it to him. He had done it accidentally and run into a little bit of trouble."

"I see. Well," Araceli replied, "a mindwalker is someone who can step into another person's thoughts, to speak, or to see what they see. It is a required ability for anyone in the Mercy, so naturally your mother was quite talented in that area. It can be a dangerous pastime when used idly, so I recommend avoiding the *shm'Ecl* until you have more control. In the meantime, if we have trouble reaching your magic through traditional lessons, perhaps we can see whether you can recreate the fluke that led you to mindwalk the first time. Assuming you intend to study, of course."

She said this in such a way that I knew she had seen my decision on my face. I nodded. I would study my magic, and then I would return to Wyvern's Court. Perhaps somewhere along the way, I could learn something that would help Hai.

"Excellent," Araceli said. "Come with me, Nicias. Lillian, would you care to assist us?"

"As you wish, my lady."

Araceli started to lead us both toward the courtyard.

When I hesitated, recalling the warnings I had been given about this yard, she turned. "Most of the city is wrapped in spells to keep you from drowning in your power before you can control it. Unfortunately, those same spells will hamper your ability to learn, until you have the conscious control to reach past them. In this courtyard, your magic will be at its strongest, stronger even than it would be off the island."

That was exactly what I was afraid of.

"You won't be able to come here without me for a while yet," Araceli assured me, "but so long as I am with you, I will be able to protect you."

I winced as the light seemed to brighten and the air warmed around me the instant I stepped onto the soft white sand.

Araceli took a deep breath, closing her eyes for a moment, and all at once I sensed the magic that she exuded. I fell instinctively into a soldier's ready, right hand grasping left wrist beneath my wings. I waited for her instruction.

"Put your hands up, mirrored to mine," she told me.

I did as she ordered, moving into what I knew only as a common starting position in serpiente dance. Arms crossed at the wrists, the backs of my hands and forearms lightly touched the same on her.

"Ahnmik's symbol is a pure white falcon, diving through a black sky. Close your eyes and see that," Araceli ordered.

I did as she said, and found that the image came easily to my mind's eye. I hoped that I would do as well here as I had elsewhere throughout my life. My parents had feared for my safety in sending me here, and if I did not return in a few days' time, they would begin to worry that I was not going to.

"I'm going to blindfold you now," Araceli said. "You are used to using your eyes. I hope to make you learn to see another way."

Her arms once again pressed lightly against mine as she tied the blindfold and returned to our original position.

"You were raised a warrior, so this exercise should be easiest for you," she said.

That was the only warning she gave. I felt the flare of her magic as if it lashed out in an attack—and I knew I had to respond.

If she had thrown something at me, my arms would have lifted to catch it. Now my magic did the same, and I had no conscious thought as to how.

I knew we never moved physically, but we might as well

have fought, danced, run, flown. The magic rippled between our still bodies.

The activity stretched until I had no sense of the world Araceli had blinded me to. There was only the power, shifting and swirling in patterns complex and simple at the same time, bright and dark, silent yet singing.

Sweat was beading on my brow, and my breath and heartbeat were racing when she finally broke contact. My body swayed with exhaustion and I stumbled down to one knee. Lily was there immediately, her touch soft and familiar as she offered me a cup full of cold, clear water. I reached up to remove the blindfold, thinking the lesson was over.

Not yet, Nicias, Araceli said. *Stand up.*

I hesitated, feeling every ache in my body all at once.

Stand up, she ordered me again.

Standing right then was perhaps the most difficult thing I had ever done, but I forced myself to obey her command. The sun, which had previously warmed the front of my body, was now an unwelcome weight on my back.

Araceli's magic struck me harder, and it was Lily's hand on my arm that held me up, even as I felt my magic sluggishly respond.

Release him, Lillian, Araceli said, sternly. *Nicias, try to push back at me.*

Tentatively, I reached out, trying to do consciously what I had done instinctively before. I managed . . . something, I thought.

Again.

I tried again, and when I fumbled, I felt Araceli's power slap across mine.

"Enough," she finally declared, pulling back. I felt a tug as she untied the blindfold; then I was blinking against the light of Ahnmik. The day had disappeared while we had been working, but the white towers glowed softly, as if reflecting moonlight that the clouds above concealed.

It felt as if the ground shifted beneath me; I braced myself against the dizzy spell, closing my eyes and breathing deeply. Araceli nodded to Lily, who came back to my side, steadying me. I flinched when she first touched my arm. My skin was badly sunburned, but it healed instantly at her touch.

Again she offered water, and I drank greedily.

"Ahnmik's magic is not gentle and its study is not easy. We will need to work on your endurance before you can master it," Araceli said. For the moment, all I desired was sleep. "I will see you tomorrow for your next lesson. For now, rest. Lillian, help him get home safely."

CHAPTER 9

LILY AND I walked toward my rooms mostly in silence. Part of me felt exhilarated by the lesson, and the memories of the shifting power. Another part felt acute frustration. Never in my life, in classes or training or any other form of study, had I worked so hard and accomplished so little. I didn't know what I had learned, if anything.

Lily put a hand on my arm, drawing me back from my bleak thoughts as we reached the doorway to my rooms.

"Careful," she said. "You've burned a great deal of power today—more than you're used to losing so fast. Sometimes it can lead to melancholy. Are you hungry?"

I shook my head. "Strangely, no."

"Not strangely," she corrected. "It's normal, especially the first few days. You will learn quickly that your magic can sustain you. But watch out; as soon as your body remembers that it requires food, you'll wake up starving."

She pushed open the door, and I followed her in, watching the lights emerge from the patterns in the walls as we entered.

"Why don't you take down your wings and relax?" she suggested. Her own wings slid against her body and faded away as she spoke, hidden until she was ready to walk about the city again. She stretched, arching her back and twining her fingers together behind her.

I did the same, but flinched as I discovered a sea of pulled muscles. They would stiffen that night and ache the next day.

"I've never worn my Demi form for this long in my life," I said, carefully rolling my shoulders to try to work out some of the kinks.

Lily winced in sympathy and moved behind me.

"If you'll lie down, I'll rub your back for you."

"That would be wonderful," I said before I'd had a chance to think the answer through.

I had been raised close enough to the serpiente that casual touch did not shock me, but I was still very avian at heart, and I had a moment of unease as I lay on the bed, head resting on my hands, with an attractive woman beside me. Even more so the first time her palms smoothed down my back.

I had never thought of Lily that way before, because neither of us had ever been available. I had always known that she would have to return to Ahnmik. And I had always been one of Oliza's Wyverns.

"You are either angry, frightened, or nervous," Lily said. "I don't think I frighten you, and I certainly hope I don't anger you."

She left unspoken the last possibility. As she sat on the bed beside me, I started to push myself up.

We *still* were not available.

Lily's gentle hands on my shoulders directed me back

down. "Relax, Nicias." Her voice betrayed the laughter she was trying to subdue. "Relax."

I took a deep breath and concentrated on doing as she said. Eyes closed, I let myself think of nothing more than the feeling of sore, tense muscles being worked out.

Beyond where her hands touched my skin, I felt a faint tickling sensation, a warm buzz that made me so calm I thought I might sink through the mattress. Magic. I recognized it, but the desire to question her drifted away.

"Much better." She sighed. Her hair swept across my skin as she leaned over my back, and I would have tensed again if I could have summoned the energy to do so.

She brushed my hair to the side, and her fingers slid through the indigo feathers that grew at my nape. "Relaxed now?"

Suddenly . . . not exactly.

And even less so when her lips touched my shoulder, silently offering and asking at the same time.

I sat up, and this time Lily did not stop me. She just flopped onto the bed, letting out a heavy breath.

"Nicias—"

"You know I have to go back to Oliza," I said. I pushed myself to my feet, wanting very much to hold Lily, but fighting not to. "I can't stay on Ahnmik. And I know you need to stay. So we can't—"

"Nicias, I'm no avian sweetheart," she said softly. "I'm not offering marriage. I'm offering companionship, a heartbeat beside yours." She sighed, her blouse stretching taut across her chest, which did not help me keep control. "You've lived so close to the serpiente, how can it still be alien to you to sleep with another life beside you?"

I took a step back, needing to put more distance between us.

The problem was that it *wasn't* completely alien to me. As a child, I had shared a serpiente-type nest with Oliza; her cousin, Salem; and a few others. I had stopped doing so before I had joined the Wyverns, but I often missed the warmth and company as I slept.

"I know I will never be first to you," she said, as if reading my mind. "You have sworn your loyalty to Oliza much as I have sworn my loyalty to the white Lady, and nothing—*nothing*—will ever precede her in your heart. Duty will forever come first to you; I admire that because it is the same for me. But loyalty does not have to displace every other kind of love. For right now, neither of us is called upon. For tonight, we can just . . . be."

There was no arguing with that.

Lily was right. Oliza had my vow. I would give my life for my queen. Until that day, however, that life should be mine to do with as I chose.

Before I could speak or make a move, Lily let out a frustrated prayer of *"Ecl* spare the girl who waits for you to make up your mind."

Then she kissed me, standing on her toes and leaning against my body. Tentatively, I let myself put an arm around her back, holding her close, and I felt her lips smile against mine before she drew back just enough to speak.

"If you want me to go, I'll go," she said, softly, blue eyes vulnerable. "But I would rather stay. And I think you would rather I stayed."

She stayed. I stayed. The night was marvelous, and I had one vivid thought before I fell asleep: *I could get used to this.*

* * *

And then I was somewhere else entirely, back upon the nightmare landscape that was now familiar to me: Hai's world. Black sand dunes appeared, frozen forever in place. Far away I could see the high turrets of a castle, but when I took a step toward them, I heard an ominous hiss.

The black cobra reared its head.

I took a step back, willing myself elsewhere, and soon found that I stood before another figure.

Darien was pacing furiously, dressed in suede slacks, vest and boots. Her white-gold hair flowed behind her, loose and wild, not quite in time with her movements.

"Before you ask," she said sharply, "yes, you are asleep. And yes, I am really speaking to you. It is difficult to do so here. You should come back to the hall where they keep me."

She paused and looked directly at me with eyes that seemed to shift color: from green, to blue, to violet, and finally to pale gray.

"I can't right now," I said, my own voice alien to me. "I'm not quite sure why I *should,* either."

"Fool child," she spat. "Trusting fool child. A woman bats her eyes at you, and you think she's harmless." She shoved my shoulders, sending me stumbling on the ice, which was suddenly slicker than before. "Another woman shares stories of how it hurt—oh, how sad she was—when she tortured her son for days and exiled him from his homeland. And you trust them both with your body, your mind, and your magic."

"Do I have any more reason to trust you? You're supposed to be mad."

Her face fell. As she sighed, a cold wind whipped across the ice, making all the hairs on my arms rise as I shivered.

"Yes, mad," she whispered. "Mad for challenging the white Lady, for daring to defy her. For daring to despise the woman your father once called mother, and your lover calls Queen. You didn't realize that, did you? When Lillian speaks of her Empress, she means *Araceli*. She is guilty of treason in her heart if not in action. If I was still sworn to my lady Empress, I would have brought dear Lily before her long ago."

"You're not endearing yourself to me," I said coldly.

She looked at me as if I had not even spoken. "But you, Nicias, you are not the Empress or her heir. You may even have some sort of a heart, despite the poison from your royal blood."

That was a rousing endorsement. "Why do you hate Araceli so?"

"Why does the cat hate a mouse?" she returned. "Why, more like, does the mouse hate a cat?" She whipped her head to the side, as if hearing something else. "Not now."

"Darien?"

"I thought no one remembered my name anymore, save Servos," she said, softly. "All those who mattered have forgotten. It is nice to hear you speak it."

Darien's eyes burned violet as she looked at me.

"A word of advice, *prince*, for your travels in our fair city. Everyone on this island is a pawn. You, me. Syfka. Cjarsa. Everyone. It's accepted; it's *expected*." She sighed and whispered, "I borrowed a feather of your soul, son of the son of she who shines in the darkness, she who glints on ice. I borrowed it and kept it safe."

"What are you talking about?" I demanded.

"I borrowed it and made it dance for me, and it said . . ." She let out a falcon's shriek that made the ice shatter in all directions. I struggled to stay out of the water underneath, but felt myself falling.

"It said, son of the son of the Lady, that you would destroy an empire."

I fell into the water and felt it close over my head before I struggled back to the surface to find Darien kneeling on a patch of unbroken ice, offering her hand.

"I could never forgive myself if I let Kel's child drown here," she whispered.

I took her hand, and she pulled me up, whispering, *Come to me, Nicias. We need to speak.*

Then I was awake, shuddering from the dream that wasn't a dream. I needed to go to her. I needed to know what she meant.

Lily snuggled against me, her eyes heavy-lidded with sleep, looking much bluer at this hour. "Something wrong?"

"No, no," I answered, perhaps too hastily. "Go back to sleep. I need to talk to someone."

She threw an arm around my waist, snuggling against my side as I tried to stand up. "It's the middle of the night. You don't need to talk to anyone right now."

"I should—"

"Nicias, go back to sleep," she said, laughing and reaching toward me to run a hand up my chest. "Or, if you don't want to sleep, I'm sure we can find a way to pass the time. But if you wander around Ahnmik alone at this hour, you're asking the roads—if not *Ecl* herself—for trouble. Whatever it is, it can wait."

I sighed, relaxing back into her arms. I didn't even know

anymore why I had wanted to see Darien. She hated Araceli and Lily, and her own daughter had shown me how dangerous *shm'Ecl* were, despite their apparent stillness. I had no sane reason to go to Darien now, and plenty of reasons to stay with Lily.

CHAPTER 10

THE NEXT MORNING dawned cool and misty—or so I was told. By the time Lily and I woke and greeted the day, most of the fog had burned off and the air was as pleasant as in springtime. I awoke to find slender silver lines along my chest and stomach. When I asked about them, Lily blushed.

She brushed a hand across the marks, making my breath catch as the magic oscillated. "Harmless," she said. "Think of them as . . . love marks. Though I can remove them if they worry you."

With her eyes that beautiful indigo, her hair still rumpled from sleep and her hands on my chest, there wasn't much that could worry me.

We bathed and dressed, then emerged into Ahnmik with the languor that always follows deep sleep. Lily unfurled her wings as soon as we stepped into the outside world, reminding me to do the same.

It also reminded me of a question. "I was told that outsiders and mongrels"—I still hesitated to say that word *quemak*, though I had accepted that the falcons used it differently—"are not allowed to wear their wings in the city, but when I saw Hai among the *shm'Ecl,* she was wearing hers."

Lily's expression was grim as she said, "The Empress favored the girl, and made an exception to the law. She regretted it when Hai became a poignant example of why mongrels are forbidden in the sky. The city is not kind to those it does not consider its own."

More say that they are imbued with thousands of years of magic from those who live here, soaked with their dreams and thoughts, and thus given a personality of their own. Lily had said that to me earlier, when I had asked whether the roads were alive. Now the memory prompted a dark thought.

"You said the city's mind comes from those who have lived here," I said. "Wouldn't that mean its actions toward outsiders are inspired by its inhabitants' feelings toward them?"

Lily laughed, shaking her head. "Oh, Nicias." Her amused tone seemed to say "You are being terribly naïve, and it's terribly cute." I found that when she looked at me with eyes that were nearly violet in the morning light, I lost my breath as well as my desire to argue.

For now, I was content to listen to Ahnmik's music and watch the people who passed, all of them wearing the wings of gyrfalcons, peregrines, aplomados and merlins.

One of the buildings we passed was a kitchen, and Lily picked out two small freshly baked bread loaves with honey for us to nibble on as we walked. I wasn't particularly hungry, but made myself eat anyway. Maybe food would fortify me, in case that day's lesson with Araceli was as rigorous as the one the day before.

It didn't—at least, not enough for me to notice a difference.

Around noon Araceli called for a break, and we sipped mint tea as we discussed things of great and little relevance.

The conversation turned to my life in Wyvern's Court. "The two civilizations aren't exactly combined," I explained. "But they've come a long way since the wars. Right now, the northern slopes are primarily avian, and the southern slopes are primarily serpiente. The two groups do gather in the market, though, and many of the younger ones share classes. The older generation has bent as far as they are able just by moving there, but their children will go further," I said confidently. "It's a slow process, but I have faith in them, and faith in Oliza to lead them."

Araceli sighed. "It's amazing to the point of frightening, those two working together."

I nodded. "My parents have told me enough stories of war to make me glad that I was born in peace."

I instantly regretted mentioning my parents. To Lily and Araceli, they were very different individuals from the ones I knew and loved.

"I remember your mother a little, from when I was a child," Lily said, tentatively. Araceli sighed and nodded for Lily to continue. "But then, watching the Indigo Choir dance is not something anyone could forget, no matter how young."

"The choirs dance?" I asked, confused.

"Each choir is a rank, and each rank is defined by how many levels of our magic its members can weave," she explained. "It takes most people centuries to master as many layers as your mother managed in the sixteen years before she fled. Kel was among the Empress's favored from the time she was seven. I remember how much I envied her for that as a child. No one ever spoke Kel's name without pride, without respect." Softly, she added, "And then she left it all behind."

I wondered if Lily shared Araceli's opinion about my mother's actions. "Do you know why?"

"No one's ever content with what they have, I suppose," Lily answered carefully. It was the same thing Oliza had said to me on my last day in Wyvern's Court.

Araceli scoffed. "Kel had earned the highest rank a non-royal peregrine can achieve in a fraction of the time such prowess usually takes. That power, along with the Empress's favor, and her fame as a dancer, gave her a great deal of arrogance."

"But how can you say—"

She put up a hand to silence me. "Your mother was always restless, but she had sworn herself as one of the Empress's personal guards. When she began to feel the weight of the duty she had chosen, she fled rather than face it."

The picture Araceli painted was so different than any I would ever have associated with my mother. It chafed so much that I couldn't help challenging Araceli. "And my father?"

I expected her to silence me again, but instead, Araceli looked away, drew a deep breath and attempted to answer me.

"First Sebastian wanted to learn about other places. I was wary of letting him go, but Syfka argued reasonably on his behalf, so I allowed him to act as a kind of ambassador to the avians. Suddenly he announced that he was in love with a hawk. It was a childhood infatuation, and if I had treated it as such, it would have blown over, but I overreacted, demanded he return home, pressured him too much. And lost him."

Both my parents sounded like impulsive children running away from home.

"I do not care for the girl I used to be," my mother had said to me once, when I had asked why she never spoke of her past. My father had said almost exactly the same thing: *"Sebastian of Ahnmik, if he had survived, was not a man I would have wanted to know."* I had always assumed that they hated their past selves due to the land that had shaped them. Was it possible that they had disowned their pasts because they *had* been as flighty and immature as Araceli described? They had grown since and learned the ideals of duty and loyalty and honor that they had taught to me. Surely they would hate remembering that they had once fled their responsibilities rather than facing them.

I was grateful when Araceli asked, "Are you ready to return to training now?"

I stood up and stretched, then answered bravely, "Anytime." I would rather be buffeted by her magic than by these dark thoughts.

Once again, we stood in the sun, my eyes blinded by what Araceli called falcon's silk—a silvery, shimmering piece of cloth that Lily had summoned effortlessly when Araceli had asked her to, weaving the fabric with nothing but air and magic.

Araceli began the same exercise we had performed the day before, this time without her arms against mine to guide me.

Good, she said, encouragingly. *Again.*

We continued, the dance performed without either of us moving.

Again.

One more time.

Nicias, Nicias Silvermead . . .

I felt myself pull back as Darien's call echoed in my mind. "Nicias of Ahnmik, focus!" That command came from Araceli.

I felt Darien slip in between Araceli and me. I was distantly aware that *she* was dealing with Araceli now, mimicking my faltering attempts at the magic to keep Araceli from sensing that anything was amiss.

Nicias, leave them and come to me tonight, Darien crooned. *If you want power, I can give you power—*

Her voice faded away, then came back sharper than before.

Nicias, you wear lines of magic on your skin. Are you fool enough to think they are harmless?

For a moment, I felt uneasy. What did I really know about falcon magic?

Tonight, Nicias, come to me.

Then she was gone, and I staggered under Araceli's magic. The blindfold was pulled away, and I blinked against the unexpected light.

"That's enough," Araceli said. "You did well. Within the next few days, perhaps, we can start working on simple Drawings."

I wasn't paying much attention to her, just nodding mechanically to acknowledge the compliment.

What if Darien was right? My mother and father had warned me about Araceli, as Darien was doing now.

But Darien was mad.

Yet she had given me very real and sane doubts. "I think I'm going to—"

Lily leaned against my side, sighing tiredly, before I could finish my sentence. I needed some time to walk around the city on my own again, but I didn't have the heart to send her away.

"If you aren't too tired, you would probably enjoy watching the dancers," Lily suggested. "Indigo Choir performs tonight."

Araceli nodded. "I know that the serpents you were raised with still dance, performing what they recall of the ancient steps, but you have never seen a true *sakkri* performed. It is a sight you should not miss."

CHAPTER 11

A S DUSK FELL, Lily hurriedly led me through the glitter-ing streets and toward the triple arches I had seen from a distance, but had never tried to locate.

"There are three arches, at different heights," she explained as we approached. "Talented air-dancers test their wings by trying to fly through the tiny space between where the arches almost intersect. I've known more than one arrogant dancer who has lost pinfeathers and pride to that trick—myself included, I admit. The air-dancers we will see tonight are all of the highest rank." She squeezed my hand. "Trust me, you will be amazed. Especially since you have only seen the dull imitations done by the serpiente. These are real."

I was about to defend the dancers I had grown up with when we passed through the veil of magic that separated the arches from the rest of the city. The air changed, cooling slightly. The music around us also changed, from the indistinct singing of the roads to the murmur of voices hushed in anticipation.

The five dancers were gathered at the center of the arches,

facing each other with their arms crossed at the wrists and their fingertips touching those of the person next to them. They stood like statues, moving only to breathe, which they did in perfect unison.

"What do you mean, these are 'real'?" I asked.

"Serpiente dance with their bodies, and that is it," Lily said. "A falcon dancer uses her body to weave magic. When the serpents perform the *daraci'Kain*, you watch and perhaps enjoy the dance. When Indigo Choir performs the *daraci'Kain*, you feel the rain on your skin. You are the thunder. The magic speaks of love, and you feel love so powerfully, you would give everything to keep it; it speaks of fear, and you shake in terror. Wait and see."

Lily's description didn't make me eager to experience this, but in that moment the last of the day faded, and the five dancers hit the first note of the music together. They were answered by the arches themselves, which began to sing as the five moved into the first steps of the dance.

The first turn left a trail of silver magic. The dancers were like shadows, silhouettes against the colorful patterns the dance left behind.

I closed my eyes for a moment and could still see the dance and the magic, ripples of silver, plum, violet, burgundy, deep sapphire and rich emerald building and hanging in the air.

Suddenly I could feel more than myself, more than the dancers; I could feel the breath of the city, how the magic was wrapped into everything—even the *shm'Ecl*. I felt pure love as the city kissed its sleeping kin.

I dropped to my knees, and I felt Lily do the same beside me. We were breathing in sync, hearts beating together. I opened my eyes and nothing changed.

There were tears on my face, and I did not brush them away.

The performers sang another note and moved into another dance, and now it was not perfect love I felt, but awe. Within a few moments, I recognized the steps of the *daraci'Kain* from serpents' performances, but as Lily had said, serpents simply couldn't do *this*.

As Lily had described, I felt the fury of the storm, and when I closed my eyes, I could feel the warm rain. I was a wave in the ocean, thrown to the shore and then drawn back out again and again.

I saw lightning, and my breath caught until a roll of thunder reverberated through me.

Still trembling from that shock of power, I felt the dance shift once more, to a *sakkri'teska*, a dance of thanks. Calming, soothing. The magic fluttered across my skin like the wings of a thousand butterflies, cooling that which the storm had scorched.

I was filled with gratitude, and again I felt tears in my eyes.

When the dance broke, I found myself on my knees with my hands splayed before me and my head bowed. I was not alone; some had bowed even lower, so that their foreheads pressed against the ground.

Each of the five dancers turned to face us and sank into a similar bow, returning the honor.

A few of the audience stood, including Lily, who stepped forward. *"Varl'nesera-fm'itil,"* she said, praising the dancers and kneeling before one of the women. You bless us, dancer.

"Fm'varl'nesera-hena," the falcon replied. Be blessed.

By the time Lily returned to my side, I felt almost capable of standing. Offering me a hand, she said, "You do the dancers a great honor by attending the performance. It is not often that any of the royal house are present."

"I'm not—"

She put a finger to my lips. "It may seem unimportant to you, but you are still the Lady's blood. It means something to those who performed for you tonight. It means much to them that you were so moved. Most of the strongest do not allow a dancer's magic to touch them. I believe they miss a great deal." Shyly, she offered, "Perhaps someday I can perform for you. I would do a *harja*, though you might accuse me of trying to use magic to seduce you."

I laughed a little, hugging her close. "Do you need magic, Lily?"

With her eyes so fair they were almost gray, she asked softly, "Do I?"

The moment hung heavily, words unsaid. She looked away first, turning the conversation back to a neutral topic. "The dancers will stay here for the next several days as they recover. It takes a great deal of energy to spin magic as they have tonight."

"I can imagine," I answered. "Was my mother really once able to do that?"

"That and more," Lily answered. "She was one of the best. I once saw her dance a *sakkri'a'she,* when I was a child. . . ." She shuddered. "A dangerous dance."

"*Sakkri'a'she?*" I asked. *A'she* meant future, but I did not know what it meant in this context.

Lily's gaze lifted, and she scanned the skies as if for inspiration. "Some of the most powerful magics are the *sakkri'sheni,* those that deal with time. Most easily, the past can be viewed—though never changed, of course. I can spin that

96

form, though it is difficult. Then there are those dances that show the future: that which might come to pass. They're unpredictable, and show unlikely events the dancer fears as often as they show nearly certain futures." Softly, she added, "No one foresaw that Kel would run."

The mention of my mother's name was jarring. My skin was still tingling from the Indigo Choir's performance. I didn't want to think about home right then.

I was enjoying Lily's company; I had even enjoyed Araceli's. I tried to keep my father's words about Araceli in mind, but that day she had seemed so different to me from the cold woman my father had portrayed. And then there was the city, its songs and its living roads. I understood now why my parents could not speak of this place without sighing.

Once Araceli had taught me my magic and I was able to safely leave, I would have to go back to Wyvern's Court. I was loyal to Oliza. I had sworn my life to her. But I was beginning to feel reluctant about abandoning all I had learned, abandoning the city and the company of both Araceli and Lily.

Oliza would want me to be happy. She of all people knew what it was to be an outsider; she would understand the appeal of a world for my own kind.

I winced. When had *my own kind* stopped meaning the avians and serpiente I had been raised with and started meaning this civilization I was related to by seemingly little more than blood?

Again, Lily drew me from my dark thoughts, hugging me as she kissed my cheek.

"I'm sorry; I did not mean to upset you, especially after a day as long as the one we've just shared."

We returned to my rooms together. This time there was

no debate. Already it felt right to have Lily beside me as I slipped gracefully into sleep—and onto the familiar black ice, lit only by the silver moon.

"The night on ice," came Darien's voice. I turned, but could not find her. "That is how *Ecl* is described. Just as Ahnmik is the white falcon, diving through the midnight sky."

I heard a screech and looked up to see the image she had described, the falcon diving . . . diving until it slammed into and through the ice, sending fractures out in a million directions, a million fingers of gray in the blackness.

"Shm'Ecl."

I felt her breath on my neck, and I turned to find her standing close, dressed in a traditional falcons' outfit like one Lily had worn earlier. Her image blurred before my eyes, and then it *was* Lily standing there.

But when she spoke, the voice was still Darien's. "Do you like this form better? Do you trust it more?"

I stepped back, unsure of how to deal with her icy rage.

"Do you notice the way her eyes change color?" Darien asked. "The magic stains a falcon's body. The magic is what puts the blue into your hair. What do you think makes her eyes violet? And why do you think you turn from your questions the instant she wishes you to?"

"I've known Lily for years," I replied. Why was I arguing with Darien? Why did I feel the need to justify myself to a specter I had never even met in the flesh?

"Two years," Darien said. "Two years are nothing in this world, especially when the prize is the trust of a royal falcon. Look at me, Nicias!" she commanded when I tried to will myself out of this dreamland. "Look at me and listen to my words with all the intelligence and reason I would expect from Kel's child."

"What do you know about my parents?" I demanded.

"Enough to know that neither of them would have fled this island if there was nothing here to flee," she retorted.

Darien turned, as if startled by something. "You don't speak of a mindwalker without her knowing, especially when you lie so close to her, but what choice did I have? Nicias, Nicias, if you want to learn your magic, I could teach you . . . everything," she whispered. I could feel the effort it was taking her just to maintain contact with me. "I could teach you in one night what it may take you a hundred years to learn from Araceli."

Come to me.

The ice shook at her command, and I was lost again, surrounded by black mountains. The serpent who had haunted me was before me again, but as Darien's voice echoed, it recoiled.

Come to me.

I pushed past the cobra, following the only path I could see as the ice began to shatter around me.

Come to me.

When I woke, it was because Lily was shaking me.

"Who calls to you?" she asked.

I blinked in disoriented surprise.

"I grasped the barest tendrils of the magic," she explained. "It is a powerful call. Who is it from?"

I answered, "One of the *shm'Ecl*. Darien, she is called."

Lily's eyes widened, and she snuggled closer to me. "I am glad I have never heard that one sing . . . not since *Ecl* took her. Be careful, Nicias, and take her words with a grain of salt. Darien hates the royal house. She was one of the Empress's Mercy, until she turned on her liege. I was there the day Darien attempted to assassinate Araceli." Lily twisted, and I noticed for the first time the faint scar under her right shoulder. "Her blade ripped through my back, into my heart. My brother saved my life. Mer fell to *Ecl* that day, but at least he took that bloodless creature with him."

I shivered, thinking of how close I had come to trusting Darien.

"That's why Darien is bound now," she explained. "Even if she recovers from *Ecl,* she won't be able to leave those halls."

"Why wasn't she executed?" There had to be more to this tale, but I didn't know what.

"The Empress is merciful . . . and she has always been very fond of Darien, despite all the traitor has done," Lily said bitterly. "Be careful. Until you learn to protect yourself, I fear that even bound Darien could wrap you in persuasion magics so strong you wouldn't hesitate to hold a knife to your own throat."

She tucked her head into my chest, and I felt a wash of guilt. Her brother's fall was what had driven her to Wyvern's Court. Now that she had returned to Ahnmik, what right did I have to make her face her demon again?

"If you will let me," she said, "I can share with you dreams more pleasant than those of the black ice."

I nodded.

As we drifted back to sleep, I thought I heard one last faint whisper from Darien.

I am not the only one on this island capable of such magics, Nicias, she warned. *Even my enemy has told you that I am bound and helpless. Now come to me.*

CHAPTER 12

THE REST of the night passed blissfully, but we had barely stepped through the door of my rooms the next morning when Lily was pulled away.

One of the Pure Diamond falcons who I had seen guarding the palace delivered the summons. "Your lady would like to speak to you."

Lily looked surprised. "Is it time for Nicias's lesson already?"

Now it was the messenger's turn to look surprised. "Your lady the *Empress Cjarsa* has requested your presence," he clarified.

Lily's eyes widened. "I apologize. The Empress so rarely grants audiences, I didn't imagine she would have reason to summon me. Nicias, I'm sorry, I must leave you for a while. Please, be careful."

She kissed my cheek and then changed shape without another word.

"Is something wrong?" I asked the Pure Diamond falcon before he could leave, too.

"I do not know the circumstances of the command, sir," he answered, watching me with an eerie focus. It took too many moments for me to realize that he was standing at attention, a guard before his monarch, awaiting either further commands or permission to leave.

"Dismissed," I said, not at all comfortable with the turnabout. I had heard that word many times from Oliza, my commander and the Tuuli Thea and Diente; I had never expected to speak it.

"Thank you, sir." He changed shape, spreading black-and-white gyrfalcon's wings to take himself back to the palace.

Only after he was gone did I realize we had had an audience. Instead of greeting me, Syfka said, "Pure Diamond falcons are bound magically to obey anyone of royal blood. That you have not decided to stay as Araceli's heir doesn't change that."

"Can I help you?" I asked, still distracted. Syfka had shown no interest in me since I had arrived on Ahnmik, but now she obviously had something she wished to say.

"Your mother left some things here when she fled," she said briskly. "Rightly, they're yours now. If you'll come with me?"

She turned without waiting for me to respond, and I hastened to follow. I thought she would lead me into the courtyard, but she passed by the white sands, and instead we went to one of the three *yenna'marl.*

"This is the Mercy's tower," Syfka explained as she led the way up a spiral staircase formed of smoky glass. We passed by several doorways, each marked with a different pattern. "And this was your mother's room. It has been locked since she disappeared."

She touched the doorway, and the patterns shifted until

the door clicked open and Syfka stepped back to allow me access.

"Thank you."

She shook her head. "If it was my choice, I would have had these things destroyed years ago. It was Cjarsa who favored Kel and Darien, Cjarsa who ignored their treason as if they were children and not guards of the royal house, and Cjarsa who commanded that your mother's possessions be passed to you." She snapped, "Help yourself," before turning and abandoning me with the remnants of my mother's old life.

I pushed the door open the rest of the way. As they did in my room, the walls began to emit a soft light. In here, the marks were not just silver, but also violet. I wondered whether my mother had been the one to create them.

Though most of the bedding had been stripped away long before, a silky shawl had been left behind. I picked it up and realized that it must be a *melos,* one of the scarves given to dancers as the highest praise for their work. It felt as light as air in my hands and shimmered with all the colors of the sky at sunset.

In one of the corners, the artist who had woven it had left a note:

a'sorma'la'lo'Mehay
ka'hena'itil'gasi'ni
la'gen-Darien

I translated the words swiftly. To the sister of my soul: a more beautiful dancer there never was. Yours, Darien.

I put the *melos* down, wondering how my mother had known this woman well enough to merit such words.

On the far wall stood a vanity made of pale birch wood. Its surface held a silver hand mirror, an assortment of hair clips and a portrait—a ghostly image etched into a glass surface.

At first I didn't think I knew either of the two women in the picture. They were both sitting on the edge of the cliffs, looking out at the ocean and laughing at something. Then I recognized my mother's violet eyes, in a falcon's face I had never known.

The other woman, I realized with a start, was Darien. She seemed so happy and carefree in the portrait, I almost couldn't believe she was the same woman who haunted my dreams.

Next to the portrait was a small box, with a hastily scrawled note beside it: *I go to confront Cjarsa today. Please keep these for me. They should go to my daughter when she is old enough to understand.—Darien*

Underneath the box was a letter, unfinished and unsigned, but in Darien's handwriting. It was a letter to Hai's father, informing him that Darien carried his child, but most of what she had written was crossed out.

A self-mocking scrawl at the bottom of the page read, *Why should I bother to tell him of a child who the Lady will never let him know? A child the Lady will never let study magic, but would rather sentence to* Ecl *for the misfortune of having her father's blood?*

Darien had trusted my mother with these things, and with her daughter's future. My mother had kept them, as well as the *melos* and the portrait, and displayed them as cherished belongings.

Darien had called to me many times, but I had never thought I had a reason to believe her words. Now I realized how close she had been to my mother, and it made me reevaluate everything Lily had told me.

I used my mother's *melos* to carefully wrap up the box of

Darien's belongings, along with their picture. I planned to take the scarf and portrait back to my mother when I went home, but the other things belonged to someone else. Someone I had just decided I should see.

✳✳✳

This time, I found the Halls of *shm'Ecl* without difficulty. Servos greeted me, but did not ask questions as I walked past him.

Shortly I began to hear Darien's voice again, a haunting singsong.

Foolish child, foolish child, you tread in power and greed. Foolish child, foolish child, you tread in blood and darkness. Nicias of Ahnmik, Nicias Silvermead, destroyer of an empire. Come to me.

Though magic held them all, Darien was the only one of the *shm'Ecl* who was physically bound. I could hear her chanting as I approached.

"Finally the great prince deigns to speak to me," she said once I stood before her. "He lets them mark his skin and use persuasion magics on him first, but finally he comes to me."

"How did you know my mother?" I asked as I knelt before her.

"Will you remove this blindfold?" she replied. "You know that sight only hampers our magic. If I wished to harm you, a blindfold would only make it easier. I would just like to look at you as we speak."

That made sense to me. I put my mother's belongings down between us and reached to pull the blindfold away. The cloth seemed to dissolve beneath my touch.

"It's falcon's silk, woven by Pure Diamond," she explained as I stared at the remnants of the fine material. "It can't be untied, removed or cut, except by one of royal blood."

She kept her eyes closed for a moment, as if bracing herself for light, and then slowly lifted her gaze, uncertainly.

I felt a rush of familiarity. When I had fallen in the woods, the silver eyes that had looked upon me, the curious voice that had spoken my name, had surely been Darien's.

"Nicias, you wear your mother's blood so visibly on your face. Even if she no longer does."

"How did you know my mother?" I asked again as Darien looked at the objects I had set between us.

She smiled a little. "Kel and I were ever rivals for the favor of our Empress. And yet we were friends, closer than any among the Mercy had ever been. Her friendship was the brightness of the life I led. Mine was the brightness of hers, I believe. But then we found ... what we did, and I fought the Empress.

"Cjarsa does not acknowledge friendship or loyalty to any but herself. Kel would have been the one to give me the Empress's mercy. She fled Ahnmik rather than put me to death the way Cjarsa would have it done. And I let *Ecl* take me, rather than give my *Empress* the satisfaction of hearing my screams," Darien said.

"What did Cjarsa do?"

"You want to know?" Darien asked, voice lilting. "Will you believe me? You will not want to believe it; I did not want to believe it. And you have lived among the serpiente and the avians, as I never did. ..."

I knew of the falcons' ancient feud with the serpiente, but Darien's anger spoke of something more tangible in our current lives. What horror could this woman know that would force her to turn on her empress and would drive my mother from these lands?

"Tell me, please," I implored her.

Darien nodded and then closed her eyes.

"When the followers of Anhamirak left those of Ahnmik in the days of the Dasi, they kept their serpiente magic. Cjarsa and Araceli, falcon priestesses of Ahnmik, worried that the serpiente, being more prolific than the falcons, and more active, would be a danger.

"So they took in a young human child and raised her, to be like themselves but different. They brought her to power, and helped make her empire as strong as that of the serpiente, their natural enemies. Then they used their persuasion magics to convince one of the serpiente to stab this leader in the back. Her name," Darien said slowly, "was Alasdair. The first avian. Her people retaliated swiftly. The avians slew the eight original serpents of Anhamirak's clan. And the war that began between the avians and serpiente has continued ever since, generation to generation of blood and hatred.

"The royals of Ahnmik will do the same again, if your Wyvern's Court grows too strong," Darien warned. "Because they know that if the slaughter stops and the two lands finally find true peace, the serpiente will regain their magic and be a threat. If your wyvern Oliza comes to the throne, they *will* destroy her—but so subtly, blame will never fall on their shoulders. So many generations more of cobra, python, boa, taipan, rat snake, mamba and viper will be lost, and so many more generations of crow, raven, sparrow and hawk will fall. Perhaps Araceli will find a new pawn, maybe the wolves.

"But the royal falcons will do it. And they leave me here, locked and bound and blinded, because they know I know, and they *pray* I will be truly lost to the void and never bare the truth to the light of day."

I wanted to shout at her, to demand that she take it all back. I had not been alive during the war, but I had heard enough about its horrors. I had seen the hatred and fear that generations of fighting had left behind. Too many people my age and older were missing mothers, fathers and siblings.

I didn't want Darien to be telling the truth, but her story made too much sense to be ignored.

No one knew how the ancient war had begun—no one except the falcons.

"My mother was aware of this?" I whispered. My ears were ringing, and my voice seemed unnaturally loud.

"Once, she was," Darien said. "But no one in the avian court would have believed the truth even if she had tried to tell them. They would not have wanted to believe. Now . . ." She shook her head. "Years ago Kel came back to Ahnmik to plead with Araceli to let Sebastian, your father, go free. She bartered her magic, her mind, her knowledge. Araceli burned from her memory the worst *and* the best. Kel doesn't remember anything having to do with those days. She doesn't remember what we learned . . . or who she learned it with. She doesn't remember the torture she dealt . . . and she doesn't remember me."

I winced, needing to look away, as if that could change anything.

"How did you learn all this about the falcons?"

Darien's gaze turned distant. "My daughter's father was serpiente. After he returned to his home, I used my magic to keep an eye on him. I saw him killed during an avian attack, and I reached out to save him. I think Cjarsa might have let me, but Araceli pulled me back. She told me not to interfere, though I could feel the avian poison—unmistakably one of Araceli's creations—burning through his bloodstream as if it was my own. In fury, I turned on her, demanding to know *why* we had to let him die, when it was easily within our power to end the avian-serpiente war entirely. She told me it was their choice, and not our place to interfere."

She paused and looked away. "I have never been as talented with *sakkri* as your mother was, but when Araceli lied to me that day, for a moment I could see the past as clearly as if it was marching before me. And I knew what she and Cjarsa had done. The vision was so powerful that we all knew, everyone who was in that room. Some of us chose to forget, or ignore. I couldn't, not with my child's father dead because of Araceli's ego."

What Araceli had done to Darien was unforgivable, but I was more horrified by what she had done to the avians and the serpiente. Wyvern's Court would forever be stained by their war, a war intentionally begun to cripple my world. For the first time in my life, I believed absolutely in evil, for there was no other word that could describe such an act.

"Confront Araceli if you need to," Darien said. "I see in your eyes that you are thinking of it. I can protect you from her persuasion magics."

Desperately, I asked, "How do I know you aren't using the same magics on me? Making this sound more . . . ."

Darien shook her head. "Because then you would never have been able to question me. If you can consider both sides of an argument, no falcon magic has been used on your mind." She admitted, "I tried to use magic to bring you here, but others did their best to keep you from me. Araceli suggested that Lily come to the *shm'Ecl* that first day because she realized that you were on your way, and she hoped that your 'friend's' presence would distract you until her meeting with Syfka was through. And Araceli has done what she could to distract you every time you have seemed inclined to return here. But now, Nicias . . . I do not think I need magic to make you see the horror of what Ahnmik's royal house began with the murder of the young queen Alasdair."

I nodded, still not sure I fully trusted her, but shocked by her story just the same. My body was shaking, a fine tremble. I needed to compose myself. Needed . . .

Needed to confront Araceli.

✳✳✳

I stumbled down the hall, away from Darien, almost running.

"Nicias, are you all right?" Servos caught my arm as I started to brush past him, and I looked at him without a tought of what to say.

"Darien is awake," I said, finally.

Servos winced as he searched my gaze. "She spoke to you directly?"

I nodded, wondering how much he knew.

"She is mad," Servos said. I was about to argue with him when he added, "But she is also very sane. Have care with her, Nicias of Ahnmik. She is an injured bear, just as likely to turn on the ones who try to help her as on the ones who hurt her."

And who is he to speak? Darien sighed in my mind. *Servos, guardian to these still halls. He has been kind to me, true. But he worshipped Ecl in his youth. The only reason she does not take him is that he already loves her darkness.*

Go to Araceli, Nicias. Soon is best.

My steps through Ahnmik were long and quick, yet at the same time they got me nowhere. It seemed that the three white towers that marked the courtyard of the Empress's palace were never in front of me no matter how I turned.

The roads fight you, Darien said. *They fight you because they know you are going to challenge Araceli and Cjarsa, and though they do not have lives per se, they protect the royal house—as the Mercy do. Luckily, you are of royal blood too. Araceli's chosen will not hasten to break you.*

As I tried to shake those dire words from my mind, I finally saw the path to the palace. I simply turned a bend in the road and it was before me, as if the roads and the city had given up protecting me or Araceli.

I pushed open the grand doors and found Lily standing at the base of the stairs, interrogating the falcon who had given her the Empress's summons.

"You *lied* to me."

"I gave you the message that the Lady Syfka gave to me. I do not know why the Empress would not see you," he said, defending himself.

"My lord, can I help you?" the other guard said, a little too loudly, as if to alert the others that I was present.

Lillian, now the youngest yet most powerful of Araceli's Mercy, Darien shuddered as Lily turned around, seeming startled by my presence. *She, Kel and I did always compete.*

I wondered just how old Lily was. She looked my age, but in a realm where most never aged after their twentieth year, that meant nothing.

Lily was nine when Kel fled the island and I fell to Ecl. Only twenty-nine now, Darien informed me. *Too young to know what she does.*

I did not mean to speak aloud, but could not stop myself from asking, "Did you know?"

Lily's eyes flashed from gray to violet. "Did I know what?" Her voice was fragile, her expression almost wounded. "Why are you looking at me as if I've drawn a knife on you, Nicias?" She stepped toward me.

She might as well have, Darien snarled. *Tell the two-faced little fowl that she deserved the knife I once managed to give her.*

Darien's fury toward this woman I cared for made me wince.

Lily put a hand on my arm. "Nicias, what's wrong?"

My stomach clenched with guilt. Darien's words were persuasive, but I had known Lily for—

Nicias, get control of yourself, Darien commanded. *She's put persuasion Drawings on your skin. Of course you hesitate to—*

She's used more than magic on me, I responded.

"Nicias . . . did something happen while I was gone?" Lily asked, fearfully. "Dear sky above, Nicias, *what is it?*"

Darien's shouting in my mind strengthened. *So what if she does like you? You're an excellent catch. You are the only male child of the royal house; you are powerful and influential and beautiful. None of that matters, because Araceli ordered her to seduce you, to make you want to stay on Ahnmik, and to keep you away from me.*

I tried to push Lily away, not sure whether to believe Darien, but shocked by the implications.

Lily held my arm. "Nicias—"

"I've been speaking with Darien," I said, allowing her to take the words as she wished.

Her eyes widened in fear. "Oh, gods, no." She stepped closer. "*Tasa'Ahnleh,*" she whispered. *Ahnleh* could mean many things, but in the form that Lily spoke, it meant all things evil. "Nicias, she could *kill* you."

"Were you ordered to keep me away from her?"

"Of *course,*" she answered vehemently. "Nicias, Darien is *dangerous*. She hates the royal house, of which you are a part. Araceli wanted to protect you—"

I recalled the words Lily had spoken two days before: *I know I will never be first to you. You have sworn your loyalty to Oliza much as I have sworn my loyalty to the white Lady . . .*

"Did she also give you other orders?" I demanded.

Lily crumbled, stepping back from me. "Do you think it was all an *act?*" she whispered.

Of course, Darien responded, though I tried to close my mind to her barbs.

"Why were you sent to Wyvern's Court?"

Had the tale she told about her brother been true at all? Or had she lied about that, too?

Lily drew a deep breath. "I told you the truth about why I visited your lands. If Araceli had other intentions, I never knew them."

That lying little fowl, Darien snapped. *I may not be privy to Araceli's commands, but I know how her mind works. You were coming of age, Nicias. Of course Araceli would have sent someone who could be a suitable mate, if you proved worthy—or could put you down, if you tried to tie yourself to a serpent or avian.*

I recoiled mentally from Darien, and physically from Lily. I didn't know who to trust anymore. Darien hated Araceli, and I did not think she would hesitate to warp the truth to get me on her side. Lily was working for Araceli, and I had no idea how far that loyalty went.

Araceli wanted me to stay on Ahnmik.

But why had she called Lily back before I had mentioned my fall in the woods to her?

Araceli knew that your power had awakened. She felt it that day in the woods, just as I did. What better way to make it easy for Lily to guide you here, without anyone asking questions, than to command she return? Araceli would not even have needed to tell Lily her intent.

Even now, the suggestion seemed contrived. I wanted to believe Lily; I wanted to erase the hurt from her violet gaze. She put a hand on my arm, and I opened my mouth to apologize.

Trust yourself, Darien snarled, fiercely enough to make me flinch. *Trust what you know to be true. And never trust a falcon whose eyes flash violet, for it means she is using the strongest of her magic. Is it so hard to imagine what for?*

How many times had I lost my train of thought when Lily looked at me with such jewel-colored eyes?

Ask one of the Pure Diamond if he can see Drawings on your skin, Darien suggested. *They cannot lie to you.*

I glanced at the two guards, who had been standing in silent ready positions throughout our brief conversation.

If they could see magic on me, did I really want to know?

Your hesitation itself is due to magic.

I turned to one of the Pure Diamond. "Could you see, if someone had used magic on me?"

The pain on Lily's face cut me inside. "You don't trust me at all, do you?"

"Of course I—"

"You think I've been using magic on you," she said. "You think . . . what? That Araceli ordered me to befriend you? *Sleep* with you? Fall in *love* with you?"

"No!" I protested, at the same time that Darien answered

viciously, *Yes, of course, save the love part. The Mercy isn't encouraged to love. It would be awkward, if she was later ordered to skin you or some such. If Lily is foolish enough to actually care for you, she will regret it when Araceli calls her.*

"What am I supposed to think," Lily said, "when you start asking Pure Diamond to read for magic on your skin?"

Try this one—Darien pushed at me, and I found myself saying words she was inventing. "I told you I spoke to Darien. I think she might have used magic on me. You might not be able to see it since she was a higher rank than you."

"How much did Darien tell you?" Lily asked, quietly. Her face held an odd lack of emotion; those gray eyes were shuttered.

"About?"

"Everything."

I had to tread carefully. "I think you know what she told me."

Lily nodded. "Darien, Kel, Mer and I found out together."

"And yet you still work for Araceli."

Lily's eyes had returned to pale blue, and the expression in them was cold as hail clouds. "Did Darien tell you what her fighting won? How many innocents were destroyed by her treason before the Empress had the heart to sentence her favorite to death? Did she tell you that Kel had to leave behind a sister and a lover when she fled the city and put herself into exile?

"Did Darien tell you that a few years ago Lady Cjarsa took pity on her and drew her from the *shm'Ecl* and offered pardon—and that Darien repaid the favor by trying to kill her? Did she tell you how many of the Mercy died or fell to *Ecl* that day, my brother included?" She insisted, "*That* is what Darien's struggle got her, Nicias. So don't look at me with disgust for refusing to wage that war."

Look what it got you, Lillian, Darien sighed.

Is it true? I asked her silently.

In part, the gyrfalcon acknowledged. *What she does not mention is that the Empress's pardon came with conditions. But that is history and this is now; that is my life and this is yours.*

"What other orders did Araceli give you, regarding me?" I asked, as gently as I could. I needed to know. Had any of it been real?

"It doesn't matter now, does it? It's over, *sir.*" She spat out the title, then turned on her heel and walked away from me. "Guards, Araceli and Cjarsa are both occupied. If you let him pass, it will be your hides."

Lily's wings were trembling slightly, betraying the tension in her body.

That morning, in ignorance, I had been happy. Part of me wanted to reach for her and push away the knowledge I had gained.

It *did* matter now, more than it ever had.

I called out as she ascended the stairs, "Araceli ordered you to keep me from Darien." Lily hesitated for a moment. "What will she do to you, knowing you failed?"

Her magic lashed back at me, making me stumble and strike the wall, every hair on my body standing on end. "I am no longer your concern, my lord. You have made that much clear." She pushed open the silver double doors at the top of the stairs and shut them behind her so hard that I heard them ring.

The Pure Diamond guards were watching me warily. Death to them if I forced myself past. Painful death, probably.

I had hurt enough people that day. I did not need to give myself more nightmares by fighting these two.

Then come back to me, Darien whispered in my mind. *Let me teach you our magic, teach you what Araceli should be . . . could be, if she didn't fear* Ecl.

CHAPTER 13

I WANTED to go *home*.

I could not undo the evils of the past, or forget the horrors I had learned. I could not undo the hours spent in Lily's arms, or forget the ice-cold expression on her face. I could not forget, though I wished to.

I did not want to be a royal falcon, a prince of this bitter island. I did not want their power. I wanted only to return to Wyvern's Court.

Araceli won't help you. Darien's voice in my mind was now gentler, almost apologetic. *She was pained by the loss of one heir. If she was less obsessed with purity, she never would have given up Sebastian. But she refuses to see a man with a crow's face as her son. She will not part with another child. She never intended to.*

Everything felt like it was crashing down around me. How could I learn to control my magic under these circumstances? I had been raised to be loyal and honest, and I did not have the wiles necessary to manage the game Araceli had begun.

I can teach you your magic, Darien promised. *If you have the courage to ride the Ecl, I can teach you.*

Darien was using me even as she offered to help me. Lillian had been manipulating me even as she'd shared my bed. Araceli had been engineering my thoughts and actions from the moment I had stepped onto this island. And Syfka... anyone who had seen my mother's belongings would have known that they would lead me to seek out Darien. Either Syfka or the Empress who commanded her had planned for me to visit the halls.

Syfka has her own agenda, though I do not know what it is, Darien agreed. *But if her plans force her to help you, and help me, then we can use her as she uses us.*

Did anyone here ever work under pure motives, or was it all a façade, layers upon layers of deception?

We are Ahnmik's chosen, and Ahnmik is god of control and power and the mind. These games are the way of our realm. Now come.

You, I replied tiredly, *want no less to use me than Araceli does.*

Certainly, Darien answered lightly. *But that being so, can we not use each other, too? You take what I teach you. I have faith that, with knowledge, you will do what I hope. If you do not . . . then perhaps it was not meant to be. I, however, will only manipulate you with the truth. Araceli has no such qualms. I will manipulate you with what is and what could be. Whether you choose to follow where I lead, or lead where I suggest, or fly another sky altogether will ultimately be your own decision.*

Come to me. Now.

✳✳✳

Servos was not present as I entered the halls and immediately walked up the winding ramp to Darien.

Without either of us speaking, I untied the bonds on her wrists and ankles. The knots that had held her for so long separated almost instantly at my touch, and Darien sighed.

Once free, she stood, stretched and unfurled strong white and black gyrfalcon wings. She let out a cry, half pain and half triumph. She stretched and flexed her magic as she had her body, and the sheer power made my breath catch before she finally turned her attention back to me.

Nicias.

Darien.

I thought for a while that I would never be free of my bonds. Many times, over many years, I almost gave myself to Ecl in order to escape this imprisoned flesh. Then I felt you, when your magic woke, and . . . remembered why I'd chosen this path. She stretched once more, arching her spine and reaching her hands above her head. *You are Kel's child,* she said, approvingly. *But I think you may be stronger than she is. You can handle what I have to teach you.*

"And what is that?" I asked aloud, for seeing her standing perfectly still while I heard her voice so clearly was unnerving.

"Magic," she answered. "Science. Religion. Whatever you call it. The void. The *Ecl*. I can teach you to ride it."

"And then?"

"Ride the *Ecl*, and it can never rule you," Darien explained. "If you go willingly, if you dance with its darkness, then you will keep your own mind. Your anchor. That will be enough to keep your magic from devouring you.

"If you are brave enough to begin."

She put her hands up as Araceli had the first day, then paused, allowing me to either mirror her or not. No more words were spoken.

I hesitated, but not for long.

I pressed the backs of my hands to hers.

Now dive, she commanded.

✳✳✳

Once again I was on the black ice with Darien, with the harsh wind ripping at our clothes and hair. The full moon was circled by rings of plum and cranberry, the only colors on the landscape.

"*Ecl'gah*," Darien said, naming the land.

Illusion.

"Those the Empress calls *shm'Ecl* are the ones who have fled from a world that holds too much, into a world where they can rest. Sometimes they do so intentionally—it only takes an instant, a single thought that perhaps nothingness would be easier—and sometimes they do so unintentionally, overwhelmed by their own magic until they forget where the real world is. They get caught by illusions, which are created by their minds to protect them from oblivion.

"Finally, even the illusions fade, and there is only *Ecl*. It is *nothing*, but it is beyond that. It is the absence even of emptiness. It is what is before existence, what is after annihilation. There is no desire to return, and even if one does find a mote of self-awareness, struggling is futile. The more you fight, the more painful the illusion becomes, until you sink back into oblivion because you cannot face what you have created."

Darien smiled softly.

Then, at a flick of her hand, the ice shattered. I tumbled into the cold water beneath, choking on it as I had in my nightmares, and struggled to remain afloat. The ice cut into my hands as I tried to grasp it.

"Fight and you will fall here," Darien snapped. *Now dive.*

I *can't.* My heart pounded as if it was trying to escape my chest, but as much as I shared its desire to flee, there was nowhere I could go.

"Nicias of Ahnmik, son of Kel of the Indigo Choir and Sebastian of the heir to the white Lady, mindwalker—Nicias Silvermead, sworn Wyvern of Honor. You can drown here, or you can dive. Make your choice. *Now.*"

If I did not follow Darien, I would be trapped here, one of the unmoving *shm'Ecl,* forever.

I let go of the ice, and then there *was* no ice, just the water, sucking me down. Neither cold nor hot, it engulfed me instantly. I forced myself not to struggle to the top and found myself sinking ever deeper.

My need for air disappeared, until I realized it had gone and I panicked, afraid to draw the blackness into myself as breath, but afraid not to just the same.

Again I was thrashing against nothing.

Calm yourself, child of Mehay. Fearing her darkness only drives you closer to her. I wasn't certain I could even call it a voice, let alone Darien's. *Let yourself fall. See where the darkness takes you.*

I imagined for a moment that I was back at Wyvern's Court, at the end of a long day of drills, and then I brought my mind further back, to my days in the dancer's nest. I remembered the exercises the serpiente taught, designed to relax one's body and mind.

A sigh seemed to brush against me, like silk in the darkness.

Why do you walk here, stranger? a familiar, resigned voice inquired.

Suddenly, in the distance, again I saw the black castle. I

was back on the ice, surrounded by dunes that began to ripple, smoothing and shifting so that no matter where I stepped I could not move closer to the distant castle. *You aren't wanted . . . not by me, anyway. Stay here long enough and Ecl will keep you. So why do you walk my kingdom?*

Abruptly I stood before a scene held in ice like a frozen tableau. In it were the triple arches where the dancers performed. Above the arches, a black-winged dancer lifted her face to the moonlight and stretched her body as if weightless. Her hair was black, but held scarlet highlights. Her eyes were closed.

I recognized Hai, Darien's half-serpiente daughter. My thoughts of the serpiente must have brought me to her—or her to me. There was no distance, no "here" anyway.

"Is this your kingdom?" I called. "Or is it your prison? Can you leave?"

Why would I want to leave? Hai replied.

I jumped back as the image before me shattered, shards of ice slicing my face and arms before they fell to the ground, where they turned into black and crimson feathers. I knelt to pick one up and found that it was broken and twisted, its edges seared.

What are you waiting for? Me to invite you in for tea? Go away. You shine too brightly here.

Ignoring the dismissal, I asked, "What do you mean, I shine too brightly?"

You—are, you've . . .

As if my question had distracted Hai from maintaining her defenses, the path to the castle appeared before me. I could see her, again, standing at the top of one of the turrets, her body a gray silhouette against the white moon.

My mother comes here, sometimes, but I can hardly see her. She is never . . . really here. She is surrounded by nothing and she is nothing. But you make all this seem fake. Illusion.

"It is."

"Don't patronize me!" Her voice reached me this time, not in my mind, but carried on the air. "I know this is illusion . . . sometimes, anyway. When nothing reminds me, when you and my mother don't barge in here and try to pull me out, I forget. But when you walk in, you shine, and then—" The ice around me glittered with a million colors, before it once again faded to black. "All my world fades."

"Why do you stay here when you know it's fake?"

She turned from me. *Why not?*

"It isn't real!"

There was a pause, and for a minute, I thought she had left, withdrawn into the palace. But finally she responded, *When you are not here, I can forget that. Color, sound, touch—I forget it all.*

Horrified, I asked, "And you're happy that way?"

Of course not, she answered, very matter-of-factly. *But at least I am not in pain.*

I reached the castle, only to find the drawbridge closed and the moat filled with serpents, all with their fangs bared as they moved through a vile liquid that stank of brimstone.

Is the real world so awful? No pleasure might mean no pain, but I had never imagined pain bad enough to make me pay that price. *There are beautiful things there. If you can't stand Ahnmik, you would be welcome in Wyvern's Court—*

The air laughed, an eerie giggling that came from nowhere and everywhere. *Wyvern's Court, yes. Beautiful, doomed Wyvern's Court. Leave now, Nicias. Before I need to kill you to get rid of you.*

I think your death would stain this world, but so will your life if you linger long . . . so leave now.

Hai—

You speak of illusions, my prince. *but you cannot recognize the truth. Go now, Nicias. Leave me to my sleep, and I shall leave you to your waking dreams.*

She pushed me away, and again the world around me faded. I fell into *Ecl* without any defenses, forgetting everything I was and had ever known.

There was only the void I drifted through—

Yet there wasn't, because there was no *I*, and the void can never be.

Occasionally I became aware of something more, something

Mehay

beautiful and horrible. *Ecl* rippled for a moment.

And then I remembered *pain.* I screamed and remembered *sound.*

I drew a breath and remembered *taste* and *smell* as I inhaled the dry air.

I remembered *sight* as the light blinded me, and I pressed my hands to my eyes.

Then a hand touched my shoulder, and I remembered comfort. "Mehay." A voice spoke, and I remembered music.

Still, I longed for the *Ecl,* wanted to reach out to it, because I knew it was near and inside it I would never know hurt.

"Nicias, stay with me."

And hearing my name, I remembered *I.*

I remembered my vows, every one I had ever made in my life.

Darien's voice seemed very loud, even though I knew she spoke softly. The smooth floor on which I knelt felt coarse against my knees, and the air in the halls was suffocating. *The halls*—we were back in the Halls of *shm'Ecl*. Again I saw droplets of my own blood on the floor beneath me, too real after the void. My arms were striped with the black and scarlet magic I had come to associate with Hai.

I didn't want to be here. . . .

I ran myself through the dancers' exercises. As I forced myself to relax, I found myself smoothing out the marks Hai had left on my skin. I realized I was doing it only when I saw the marks begin to fade, and I was so startled that I snapped my gaze up to Darien.

She smiled tiredly. "You have touched *Ecl,* and yet you have returned. If ever again you embrace her, you will be able to find your way back. Fear is what drives you into the darkness, beyond where any voice can reach. Relax your mind, and you will be drawn back toward this world like rain to the earth.

"Without your fear in the way, and with your royal blood to guide you, you will quickly learn how to use your magic with finesse. Simply put your body in balance, close your eyes and focus on the intent. If the spell is within your grasp, you will be able to see the pattern. Depending on the complexity, it may take you minutes to memorize, or centuries. Even if you never learn more than I have given you, it will be enough to keep you from drowning in the void."

"If what you have taught me is such an effective way to keep someone safe," I asked, "then why doesn't everyone use it?"

Darien shook her head. "And deprive the Lady and her heir of so many years during which they can brainwash their subjects?" she said bitterly. "Truthfully, most falcons discover their power when they are still children, some before they are four, and hardly any after their ninth year. But, Nicias, you are nearly a grown man. You have a lifetime of bonds holding you to this world, vows you've made and connections you've forged. Even more important, you are old enough to have a strong image of who you are. A child lacks all that. They would never have the strength to return from the void if they dove in as deeply as you and I have," she said sadly.

"Why do you sound pained?"

She sighed. "Mehay is pain, inasmuch as pain is part of existence."

"There's more to it," I pressed.

"I, too, have bonds here," she said, her gaze distant. "Vows I made in blood and magic, which lock me to this world and will for all eternity. Particularly, they tie me to the Mercy. That is a group you leave only in madness or in death."

"My mother left."

"She left physically," Darien said, "but it was not until Cjarsa stole her memories that she was truly free. It is a bit death, a bit madness."

"What pains you now?"

"When one of the Mercy feels pain," Darien said, "all do."

I knew who she meant before she said the name.

"Lillian, of the Elite Silver Choir, Mercy to Araceli," Darien whispered, "I am sorry. But Araceli put you in my way to Nicias, and I could not spare you."

"Why is she being punished for my actions?" I demanded. "I may not like the job she was given, but she did it. She obeyed Araceli. She did everything she could. I am the one responsible—"

"You only as much as I," Darien said. "Neither of us holds as much blame as Araceli. She gave the orders."

"What is happening to her?" No matter where the blame fell, I felt the guilt.

"If you want to see, reach into the Now and look," Darien snapped. "*Sakkri'equa*. That is within your power, *Nicias'ra'o'aona*. Follow your own blood. Your father's mother is with her."

It was easy.

Too easy.

I thought of doing it, and it was done. I stood—immaterial, helpless to act—by Lily's side.

There was no sound. Lily uttered no scream and gave no pleas for lenience. Instead, what seemed to grip her was sweeping despair at her failure.

She knew she would survive this.

To her, that more than anything else was agony. She had disappointed her lady Araceli. How could she ever stand to face her again, knowing that she did not deserve Araceli's forgiveness?

Her infinite mercy.

Beside me, I could feel Darien struggling with her own memories, her own feelings of guilt when she had first failed her Empress Cjarsa. There had been no torture then, but I sensed that she might have preferred it.

I tore myself away from the scene, almost back into the *Ecl*, where there was no suffering or guilt or fury. Lily had betrayed me for a monarch who had repaid her loyalty with . . . this horror.

Darien's voice reached me just before I crossed into the void, commanding, "Never flee to it. *Ecl* asks a price when you use it. You do not want to enter it to hide from pain—not if you want to return complete."

This she knew from experience.

"Always enter *Ecl* willingly, and without demands," Darien advised. "Then it will never hold you. If you seek to abandon your senses, you will lose your soul and self as well."

I nodded mechanically and then turned when I heard a swiftly indrawn breath behind me.

"Hello, Servos," Darien said.

Servos nodded respectfully, as if it was perfectly natural for him to be greeted by a woman who had previously been bound and lost to the void. "Darien." He looked at me and said, "It has been three weeks since you first came here. We had given up hope that you would wake."

"Three weeks?" I gasped. I had thought hours, maybe a day, but not *weeks*.

"You spent much time in the *Ecl*," Darien explained.

"Araceli thinks you are lost," Servos said.

How many people thought the same? After all I had experienced in this land, I finally understood why my parents had doubted I would return. Were they now convinced that they would never see me again?

What about Oliza? She would not believe that I had abandoned her—would she?

"Darien, would I survive off Ahnmik if I left now?"

She frowned. "Your magic would not kill you."

I nodded, grateful.

Darien, however, did not leave it at that. "Then you are going home now?"

"If Araceli does not try to stop me."

"Araceli does not visit these halls," Servos said. "If you

can work illusions to hide yourself, you could leave and no one would be the wiser."

"Why wouldn't you tell them?" I asked.

"I've been the guardian of these halls for too long," he answered. "I wish this madness on no one, and I wish Araceli's mercy on no one. If you stay here, likely you will suffer both." After a moment of contemplation, he added, "And I would hate to see the destruction of two who are so deft in managing *Ecl*'s swift currents. *Mana'Ecl*. Masters of the void. The title is rarely given these days, with Cjarsa and Araceli valuing mindwalkers and weavers of *sakkri* more highly, but both of you have earned it. Now . . . I will leave you two to your own futures."

Darien nodded as he retreated.

Then she demanded, "Nicias, knowing what you do, you are just going to run?"

"I have no reason to stay."

She looked appalled. "Return to Wyvern's Court and you will be just another bird, your talent and power wasted. You will not be able to use your magic lest Araceli sense it and drag you back here. You will never be able to take a mate, because Araceli *will* know if you have a child, and if it is half outsider, she will kill it. You could do so much here, *be* so much. You could be—"

"Prince," I interrupted her. "I did not want that power when Araceli offered it to me, and I do not want it now."

"But you could fight in ways that I never could," Darien argued. "And still you will not even confront Araceli?"

I met her gaze and asked bluntly, "Could we win if we fought her?"

"You are Araceli's grandson. You are perhaps the only one who *could* challenge her, could show the world what she has done—"

"And if we did *win,* what would the reward be? Would we destroy Ahnmik? What would our rebellion win us?"

"Justice to the falcons," Darien answered. "For creating a race designed to slaughter. For murdering any who could compete with them."

"You're talking about vengeance," I argued, "not justice."

She let out a frustrated screech that drew Servos back. Turning to him, she said, "You know what Araceli and Cjarsa have done. How can you live with them?"

"I am aware of their experiments," Servos admitted. "However, I am also aware of their motivations. You may want to ask Araceli about those someday."

Darien laughed, a sharp and biting sound. "I was Cjarsa's Mercy, not the Empress herself. Those two answer only to themselves."

"They would explain themselves to Nicias."

It was my turn to argue. "I don't want their explanations. I won't fight them unless they try to harm Oliza, but I won't listen to any defense for what they did. Araceli has manipulated me too many times already."

Servos sighed. "As you wish. Fly with grace and luck, Nicias Silvermead." He changed shape and departed.

"You were raised among the warring two," Darien said, "and yet you aren't even going to challenge the woman who orchestrated their ancestors' deaths?"

"I am not willing to lose my life for my pride," I answered calmly. "Why should we sacrifice more lives to avenge the lives we lost before?"

"If the avians and serpiente knew what she did—"

"Wyvern's Court is prepared to defend itself if falcons try to interfere. If Araceli was not lying, then most of her people cannot even leave this island. If we take a stand here, we will lose. But if we take a stand only on our own land, and only if forced, then we have a chance."

She frowned, but did not argue.

"I was raised a warrior," I said softly. "Any in my position would do the same. The avians and serpiente just ended their war; they want to forget, not rehash old wounds, and the last thing they want is to start another battle."

Darien paced anxiously. For the first time, I noticed the clothing she wore, which had once been very elegant, but now held fine particles of dust. "I will stay here. Maybe I can't win the fight, but for me, this is home even if it is a hated one."

"Araceli will demand that you be turned over to the Mercy the instant you leave these halls."

"Araceli will demand it, yes," Darien replied without seeming to care. "But I am sworn to Cjarsa, and so it is Cjarsa who will decide upon my sentence. If I can remain calm this time, I believe I can convince her to pardon me." Softly, she added, "If I can't, I will make sure that they kill me instead."

"That is your choice," I said, chilled by the simple determination in Darien's voice. "Though, if you would not endanger my people, you would be welcome in Wyvern's Court."

Darien just scowled and started down the ramp.

I hurried after her, wanting to say goodbye in a friendlier way before we parted.

"I told you I would only offer you the truth," Darien said when I caught up to her. "You don't agree with me. At least you don't agree with Araceli. That was my first fear, that Kel's child would turn into a creature like—"

She stopped abruptly, and all the color drained from her face. She took a trembling step forward and then fell to her knees in front of the battered young woman who had commanded all of her attention: Hai.

"My beautiful daughter," she whispered as she drew the girl into her arms, careful not to crush the magic-burned wings. "I never saw her dance. She was only an infant the last time I . . ." She shook her head. "Except for dreams in the void, I have never even seen my own daughter. I knew she was here, so vulnerable, but I could never . . ."

"I spoke to her," I said. "In those moments in *Ecl*, somehow I spoke with Hai."

Darien smiled, though it was obvious that her thoughts were far away. "Royal blood calls strongly to *Ecl*'s chosen. And you are not only a royal-blood falcon, but sworn to the Cobriana. If anyone could reach my daughter, it does not surprise me that it would be you."

"Isn't there some way to save her?"

"She has no reason to come back," Darien admitted after long, painful moments. "Her magic will always burn her, because of her mixed blood—and this city and its inhabitants will always hate her because of it. She loved to dance and she loved to fly, but these injuries have stolen both those passions from her." She touched a gentle hand to her daughter's crushed black feathers. "I don't know what either of us could say that would give her any reason to return."

There were tears in Darien's eyes when she finally looked at me, but behind them was a fragile hope.

"I can help you return home, Nicias, without Araceli even knowing that you are gone. Once I come back here, I will do all I can—and if I do win a place by the Empress's side again, I will be able to do much—to veil you from Araceli's senses in the future. Otherwise, she will notice your absence swiftly no matter how quietly you leave. All I ask is that you take my daughter to Wyvern's Court with you. I don't think she will wake; there is too much pain for her in this world. But maybe being among her father's people can help her more than I ever could."

I nodded, though it chilled me to realize that Darien never would have offered her help if she had not desired this from me. What she didn't understand was that I would have agreed to take care of Hai without receiving anything in return. Darien was very much a product of this land.

"I will do what I can for her."

CHAPTER 14

DARIEN WRAPPED the three of us in illusion, saying, "Watch and remember what I do," but warning that I would probably not be able to follow her Drawings beyond the first layers.

She was right. I could understand the pattern that hid us from view, and I thought I might be able to recreate it with practice.

After that, as Darien wove spells to fool each sense, I was lost.

I ended up sitting on the floor of the hall, Hai next to me, for I did not know how long. Sometimes it seemed that time dragged, and others it seemed that it was moving quickly. There was no way to tell. Nothing moved but my own breath. Even the signs of life that every creature emits seemed frozen in Hai and Darien.

Finally Darien gasped, her eyes opening.

They were not the liquid silver I had become used to, but indigo so dark it was almost black. She hesitated, struggling to focus.

Now, Darien said, *I need your help. Servos will not betray us, and Cjarsa never looks at the skies anymore. Araceli and Syfka are in conference.* She paused, then commented absently, *They have conversed often of late, though when I stood by Cjarsa's side, they hated each other.* She shook her head, turning her attention back to the present. *I can hide us from the Mercy, but I cannot conceal us from the Pure Diamond without your help. They are sworn to the royal house. If I use your power, I can command them not to see us, and they never will.*

That was all the warning she gave before she sent me gasping to the floor, weaving my power into her illusions to veil us from that last threat.

Eons later, she stepped forward and helped me to my feet. She handed me a small soft bundle—the belongings I had rescued from my mother's old room. Then she knelt again and lifted Hai into her arms.

"We will need to fly in Demi form if we are to carry her," she said, mentioning nothing of the time that had passed or the effort either of us had put forth. "It will not be quick, but we won't be seen—at least, not as what we are. We may appear to be clouds or swift-flying birds or shadows—what people expect to see when they look at the sky. Once we reach Wyvern's Court, we will be avians, familiar and unthreatening. The illusion will hold long enough for us to do what we must."

I nodded, hoping she was right.

*** * ***

How we made that flight home I do not know. Demi form is not well designed for swift or sustained travel, so it took us far longer to cross the ocean than it would have if we had been in pure falcon form. Without sleeping, eating, speaking or touching land, we flew for nearly six days.

Sometimes it seemed I was far away from myself, only dimly aware of the beating of my own wings. Sometimes I felt every aching muscle, every breath in my lungs.

By the time we reached Wyvern's Court, I was so tired that it took all my energy to guide Darien and myself to the Rookery. I knew only that I needed to check in with Oliza and let her know I was home safe.

My legs collapsed under me the instant my feet touched the familiar ground. Beside me, Darien wavered for a moment before one knee went out and she fell into a trembling kneel, Hai held protectively against her.

Though Darien's magic should have kept anyone from noticing us while we were in the air, we had definitely been spotted. Almost immediately, I saw a familiar wyvern diving toward me from the skies. An equally familiar sparrow followed her closely.

My magic cannot conceal a loyal guard from the one to whom he is sworn, Darien said apologetically. *Nor could I possibly hide myself from the woman who used to be my partner in the Mercy. Though perhaps it is best that the first to see us home are your queen and your mother.*

Once my mother returned to human form, she protested to Oliza, "I think it would be best if you would allow me to call for your Wyverns."

"The best of my Wyverns is already here," Oliza replied sharply.

Darien observed with dark humor, *It seems my magic has not failed to hide you from Kel. If we were still the friends we had once been, she would have laughed when she realized what a fine prank I had managed. . . .*

I pushed myself up, wincing as I discovered that my whole body ached, especially my back and shoulders. I withdrew my wings carefully and struggled to present myself to both my monarch and my mother.

For a moment I saw Darien's look of confusion, and I clarified, *Most don't wear their wings openly here.*

Of course, your land with serpents and hawks. Her wings rippled and disappeared with far more ease than mine had.

My mother drew her blade then and stepped between us and Oliza.

"Kel!" Oliza shouted. "Stand down."

My mother stepped back a pace, but not quite behind Oliza.

Darien had fallen back into at-ready, the respectful position of submission. With the off hand gripping the wrist of the weapon hand, it left her physically defenseless.

When Darien spoke, her voice was soft with resignation. "Kel of Ahnmik, Indigo Choir, mindwalker, beautiful dancer and once Mercy to the Empress, you don't recognize me, do you?" She spoke my mother's title in her native tongue, then switched to the language of my home, perhaps in deference to Oliza.

"I don't use that title here," my mother said curtly. "And I do recognize you, vaguely. Enough to recall that you, too, were among Cjarsa's Mercy. It's unusual to see one of that group off the island, but when it happens, it is never good."

"You are here."

She stiffened. "I am an exception. You still wear your falcon form."

"Only to you," Darien sighed. She held out her arm, palm up, displaying a very faint scar on the underside of her right wrist. A symbol of some sort. "Do you recognize this?"

My mother rubbed absently at her own wrist, but she didn't speak.

Oliza stepped forward, greeting me formally as she took command of the situation. "Nicias Silvermead, please report."

My mother frowned, and I saw her eyes widen. She had looked at me before, but Darien's magic had kept her from truly *seeing* me until Oliza had called me by name. I wondered how my connection to my mother could be less strong than the connection she shared with a falcon she barely even remembered.

"Nicias?" she whispered. Her blade lowered a fraction, but then she strengthened her pose.

I swallowed tightly, watching my own mother face me with a bared weapon. "Mother, I'm—"

She brought her weapon up as I tried to move closer, and I saw in her the lessons she had taught me many times. Defend those you are sworn to defend. Do not let yourself be deceived by what you wish to see. Err always on the side of caution. She still did not know whether I was an enemy or her own son.

I looked at Oliza. If vows of loyalty were what made the magic shiver, then perhaps this would help.

"*You* know me, Oliza," I said. "And I know you. I know that although the young men who court you give you exotic, spicy perfumes, you wear only the mild scent of almond that your mother gave to you. I know that you love to stay up all night listening to the wolves sing. I know that you dream of flying from this place and living in some faraway land." I went to one knee, looking up at my monarch the way I had when I had first gained my title as Wyvern of Honor. "I am sworn loyal to you and would swear the same again."

My mother's blade wavered.

"I know you, Nicias," Oliza said. "I never doubted who you were."

"And the woman with you?" my mother asked.

"Would like to see the Empress rot," Darien replied, causing my mother's eyes to widen. "And you know none loyal to Ahnmik would speak such, even in an attempt to fool you. I was your own partner in the Mercy, Kel—Darien, of the Indigo Choir. I know why you left, though you do not. I would never harm you."

My mother hesitated, but she sheathed her weapon. "That being so . . ." She glanced at me. "What are you doing back here? I hate to say it to my own son, but if Araceli and Cjarsa are hunting you, you bring grave danger."

Though I would rather have heard assurances of safety and a mother's love at that moment, I understood her concerns. Darien answered for me. "They aren't hunting us. They think Nicias has been lost to *Ecl,* an illusion I am happy that they maintain, and I am here only long enough to see your son and my daughter safe; I will return to Ahnmik long before anyone notices I am gone."

She spoke simply, and I knew that the impassive words were all my mother heard. She could not feel the regret and sudden, sweeping loneliness that I sensed from Darien as she looked at a woman who had once given everything to save her.

"Your daughter?" Oliza asked.

Darien stepped back, to kneel by Hai's side. "Oliza Shardae Cobriana, may I present *quemak'la'Hai'nesera . . .* Hai, daughter of Anjay Cobriana, late Arami to the serpiente."

Oliza's uncle. I had known that Hai was a cobra, but I had never had a moment to wonder who her father was. For an instant, I was washed by fear. Darien had shown herself to have many motives, none of them selfless. Had I brought home with me a pretender to the throne I had sworn to protect?

Darien dispelled some of my fears as she added, "Her condition, unfortunately, is likely irreversible, but I hope Wyvern's Court may at least make her dreams warmer than they would be on the island."

Oliza nodded, looking as dazed as I felt.

"Kel, please go with Darien and see that suitable arrangements are made for Hai's care," Oliza commanded.

"Are you certain—"

"Anjay Cobriana was my father's older brother," Oliza said, sharply. "By law, that would make this young woman Arami before either Salem or me. Circumstance denies her that birthright, but regardless, she is a cobra, she is family, and she is one of my people. If we deny Hai the sanctuary of her rightful home then we are no better than the empress who turned her out.

"Dismissed, Kel. Take care of my . . . cousin. I wish to speak to Nicias alone."

"As you wish, my lady," my mother replied, subdued. "Nicias, I hope I will have a chance to hear your story soon."

Darien gathered Hai into her arms, along with the bundle of belongings we had brought back with us. My mother's gaze fell on the *melos*, and she frowned, as if it seemed familiar. Then she nodded at the doorway, indicating that the falcon should leave Oliza's presence first.

She knows she should remember me, Darien sighed. *She wonders why I am one of the memories the Empress so carefully removed from her mind. She starts to reach for them . . . and then pulls back.*

As soon as they had left, Oliza sighed and leaned back against the wall. "Nicias . . ." She shook her head and began again. "I would like to question that girl's parentage, but it is as clearly written on her face as mine is. Anjay is the only cobra who ever traveled to Ahnmik. He returned only hours before he fell to the war. Looking at this girl now is like looking at a ghost . . . a ghost from whom I seem to have stolen a throne. What is wrong with her?"

Now the questions began. This one would be the easiest.

"The magic the falcons use makes them susceptible to something they call the *shm'Ecl*; Hai's serpiente blood makes her even more vulnerable. I don't know how to explain it, except to say that Darien was telling the truth—it is very unlikely that Hai will ever recover." Addressing the worries that had crossed my mind, I added, "Know that she has been raised as a falcon. In the unlikely event that she wakes, I doubt that she will want to acknowledge her serpiente blood, and even if she does, your people love you. They know you. They would never support a stranger as their queen before you."

Oliza nodded slowly. "Honestly, this silent cobra is the least of my concerns. There have been three fights in the market since you left, all between serpiente and the avians. I fear that perhaps my hesitation to declare my mate and take the throne is hurting my people, and keeping them apart."

This was the moment when I could say, "I learned on Ahnmik what caused the war." I could tell her what Darien had told me, that the old war and the hatred we still battled had been specifically engineered. I could tell her, and then I would no longer have to hold the dark knowledge alone. But what would that solve?

Oliza was my queen-to-be, to whom I was sworn, and she had for many years been my friend. I had vowed to protect her, and to protect Wyvern's Court, and I would. Sharing this with a people who had only come together now that they had forgotten it would be an evil I did not want to commit.

If anyone could heal the schism that falcon magic had created, it was Oliza.

"Fights in the market are still only fights; they aren't battles," I assured her. "We have come a long way. When you take the throne, you will move this land even further along."

"Soon," Oliza whispered. "I need to speak to my parents. They should know who Hai is . . . and if ever I have needed advice from them, it is now." She hesitated. "Nicias," she said nervously, "do you plan to remain among my guard, here at Wyvern's Court?"

"Of course," I answered. "If you'll still have me."

"Of course," she answered, as quickly as I had. "It's just that I wonder—now that you've seen what you have of the world, and with your magic—whether you'll be content. I want you to know that if you do ever choose to leave, I would not fault you for it. Wyvern's Court is a very small piece of the world you have access to."

Chilling was the thought that if she had said this to me before I had left, I might have taken her up on it. Without my vows to Oliza making me hesitate, how much more open would I have been to what Araceli offered?

"Either way, you should get some rest before you report to your commander. You still look exhausted."

I wondered if she was giving me time to change my mind if I wanted to.

The freedom did not comfort me.

✳✳✳

I returned to my home, intending to follow Oliza's advice, only to find Darien there settling Hai into the spare bedroom.

"Hello, Nicias. I assured Kel that you would not mind having Hai near you," Darien said. "Of anyone in this land, you best understand what is wrong with her, and the little that can be done."

I nodded. Even though the idea of Hai living in my home, forever still and silent, unnerved me, I could think of no one else I would trust with her care.

"I must leave now," Darien announced. "I am too tightly bound to the white land to leave it for long." She sighed. "And I have no place here. I envy your mother's freedom, but I cannot stand to look at her as what she now is, and have her look at me as a stranger. She has assured me that Hai will be taken care of, as much as one so deep in *Ecl*'s realm ever can be." She paused, then said, "The magic on you will fade in time no matter what I do. If you wish to remove the illusion spells earlier, I am sure you will be able to."

"What is it you plan to do on Ahnmik?"

She raised a brow. "Commit treason, naturally, with no less than the Empress's blessing." She smiled wickedly. "This is a suggestion I do not make lightly," she added more seriously, "but if ever you return to Ahnmik, you could yet claim your place as Araceli's heir. Return to the center, and see what you can do from there."

I shook my head. "It isn't my world. I won't join it to change it."

"Pity. I will probably not see you again for a long while. Don't forget me."

Forget this falcon? For better or worse, I could not imagine ever forgetting my encounters with Darien. "I won't," I vowed.

"If something does go wrong, and Araceli finds you gone, I will do my best to warn you, so that you will have time to flee Wyvern's Court before the falcons come for you." Unexpectedly, she hugged me. "I borrowed a feather of your soul once, borrowed and kept it safe," she whispered in my ear, as she had during our first meeting. "It told me that you would destroy an empire. Perhaps that empire was not the white towers of Ahnmik or the walls of Wyvern's Court. Perhaps it was the black castle of *Ecl'gah*. If you ever do manage to wake my daughter, call to me, please."

Goodbye, Nicias.

The last words floated back to me like an afterthought as Darien disappeared out the door. I watched her form shimmer into that of a beautiful black-and-white gyrfalcon and slice through the sky like an arrow.

Goodbye.

CHAPTER 15

KNOWING THAT I had done my duty—reporting to Oliza and ensuring Hai's safety—I was finally able to relax. I could barely stay on my feet long enough to reach my own bed, where I collapsed, still fully dressed.

I fell instantly into soft, sleek oblivion.

I dreamed of a beautiful dancer, with wings as black as night. She performed on a dais in the center of Wyvern's Court, so beautiful and yet achingly lonely.

Around us, the day began to dawn, warm and golden. Her eyes were closed, but she shuddered when the first light touched her.

Abruptly, her eyes shot open, as if she had just realized where she was—not in her dreams, but in mine. She turned to me with an angry hiss.

The world shattered, and I threw up my arms to protect my face—

***

Again I woke with blood on my skin, though the marks were not as bad as they had been in the past. At least this time Hai had been pulled into my dreams, instead of the other way around.

Over time I hoped I would be able to protect myself from her better as I slept. For now I did what I could to heal the marks she had left behind—both the cuts and the visible black bands.

Though I had not been hungry before, I was suddenly famished. Lily had warned me that this would happen.

The thought of her was like a knife in my stomach. I forced it away as I dressed and stepped out of my home.

After I ate, I would try to remove Darien's illusions from myself, and then I would seek out my parents. After that, I would ask my commander's permission to return to my post.

***

For now Darien's magic was still hiding me, and walking through the market as a nondescript avian man was an unnerving experience. I smiled and chatted about the weather with the merchant who sold me my breakfast, and then I continued through the crowds.

For the first time, I wasn't an outsider, a falcon in a realm of serpents and avians. I wasn't known as a Wyvern of Honor, one of Oliza's personal guards.

A group of avians were gathered near the majestic statue that marked the center of Wyvern's Court, talking quietly among themselves. They nodded polite greetings to me as I passed, then continued to speak.

"—but imagine, my son on a dancer's stage," one woman was saying. I slowed slightly, to listen. "Naturally, his father would have forbidden it outright, but I thought it best to let the boy try." She shook her head, making a *tsk-tsk* sound. "I worry for him, but you have to let them out of the nest someday. A more dignified pastime would have been my preference, but he just tells me I'm old-fashioned when I say things like that."

"Boys will be boys. He'll come home soon enough. Though let me say, I am relieved to see that our princess's interest seems to be focused on a young man with nicely traditional values," one of the women replied. "I saw her with Johanna's son Marus the other day. They make a simply splendid couple. He's just the type to help her settle down."

The conversation was drowned out by a pair of serpiente. The two were laughing so hard at something that they had thrown their arms across each other's shoulders just to remain standing. The three avian matrons glanced at them disapprovingly.

"Jaye, I've been looking all over for you," someone said, grabbing my arm.

I turned to him, sure he had mistaken me, and for a moment my head spun. Out the corner of my eye, I saw a wreath of falcon magic, and inside it a fair, slender young man with pale violet eyes. As soon as I was looking directly at him, however, the illusion of an avian youth returned.

He pulled me away from the crowd, and I went willingly, curious. As soon as we were away from the group, he asked softly, "Who is the black-winged dancer?"

What? I thought, mute with shock.

You're not the only one hiding here, the stranger said. *Now tell me who the black-haired dancer is. She was dreamwalking last night, and it wasn't pleasant for any of us. You're the only newcomer here, so it seems likely that you might be responsible.*

I did not know or trust this young man. I wasn't about to confide in him about Hai. I tried to change the subject instead. *Others are here?* He had to be talking about falcons.

We had left the crowded areas, and he returned to normal speech. "You're here. Why should it surprise you that others are, too? Though I will admit that I had been worried. I had heard that the Heir had bound her, to stop her from helping others flee the island. No one else has come here in years."

"Her?"

He gave a long-suffering sigh. "Darien. I can see her magic on you. I would not have spoken to you if I hadn't."

So Darien had smuggled a couple of falcons out of Ahnmik over the years. It did not surprise me. But the knowledge did make me a bit more at ease with this stranger, enough so to answer his question.

"The dancer is named Hai," I answered. "She is Darien's daughter."

He winced. "She is lost, then?"

I nodded. "Darien says royal blood might call to her strongly enough—"

The falcon snarled a curse. "True, but the royal house does not risk itself by wading into the void. The blood of royals may be strong with magic, but it's very thin when it comes to compassion."

Clearly Darien's magic had not completely failed to hide me. This stranger knew that I was a falcon, but he did not know that I was Nicias, Araceli's own grandson.

He continued to vent. "Even Servos, the guardian of the

halls, will *watch* them for a million years more before he ever considers trying to save one of them. Darien is the only one I've known who is brave enough to swim the still waters, but even she is barely strong enough to keep from drowning. It cuts her every time she tries."

He shook his head as if to shake loose a dark memory. "I wish I—any of us—could walk the *Ecl'gah* like Darien can. Maybe we could bring Hai back to her. Nothing less could possibly repay her for all she has done." He sighed. "If wishes were feathers, vipers would fly. None of us share Darien's talent in the *Ecl,* or her ability to mindwalk. We'd need both to even seek Hai out."

There was a moment of silence as we walked farther, toward the primarily avian section of the area. I spent it considering this new information. I had thought that Darien's fight on Ahnmik was active. It had not occurred to me that her "treason" consisted of smuggling others into Wyvern's Court or rescuing them from *Ecl.*

"I must get back to my shop," the falcon said. "If you have a few moments, many of us gather there at midday for lunch; I could introduce you to the rest."

"Thank you." The temptation to meet others who knew the place I had fled, and who understood what it was to be a falcon in this land was overpowering. "If I'm not imposing, I would be honored."

"Never imposing," he assured me. "Hiding who you are gets lonely, and loneliness is the fastest way to join the *shm'Ecl.*"

My guide knocked on his own door. A petite girl, with blond hair tumbling loose across her shoulders, barely silvered in the front and showing no hint of blue or violet, answered the door.

She stepped back warily after recognizing my host, watching me with open distrust and revealing two others: a woman tending the fire across the room, and another young man who had yet to acknowledge my entrance.

"Who's he?" the woman by the door asked.

"Darien's newest, apparently," my host replied. "And he brought Hai with him."

I offered my hand. "I haven't introduced myself—"

"Not to be rude, stranger," the woman replied, "but I would prefer not to know. The less I know, the less valuable I am, the less of a danger I am to the Lady, and the less reason she has to find me. Understand? So don't tell secrets here, and that includes who you are. Just be content that we know the white city as you do."

I hesitated, debating whether I should leave. I craved this company, but these people would not be so welcoming if they knew who I was.

"Pardon my friend's melodrama," my host said, chuckling. "She's been the most affected by the black dancer's dreams. It's true we don't share the names we were known by on Ahnmik here; no need to give that away in case one of us was found. But I'm called Gren in Wyvern's Court. That is Spark. Maya was the charming young lady who greeted you first, and that sullen fellow in the corner is Opal. That done with, would you care for anything to eat, or drink?"

"Gren, why are we being so polite to this stranger?" The question came from Maya, who was eyeing me warily. "We know nothing about him."

"He wears Darien's magic," my host answered. "That's enough for me."

"He also wears some other magic," Opal broke in. "Or am I the only one not blind to that?"

Gren frowned. "Don't try to make trouble again here. I won't have it."

Opal stood up and walked through a back door without a word, leaving his companions shaking their heads.

"Opal is not the friendliest of us," Gren said, apologetically. "But considering our situation, his suspicion is natural."

"Your situation . . . Hasn't anyone ever considered speaking to Oliza and asking her *permission* to be here? I'm certain she would grant it, and then you wouldn't need to hide so much—"

"Ask protection from the near-queen of a civilization on the verge of suicide?" Spark laughed. "Obviously you haven't been here long. No one knows who will rule next, or if this court will even still exist. It has already segregated, avians on one side of town, serpiente on the other. I've heard the dancers threaten to leave Wyvern's Court if it's true that Oliza plans to make that crow Marus her king. Of course, those threats are no worse than the ones started by avians a while back, when it seemed Oliza might choose a serpent. The turmoil makes it *possible* for us to hide, and we're grateful for that, but when the wyvern chooses her mate, she may well push this world back to war—and you should never trust yourself to someone who might be powerless."

Her matter-of-fact words were a kick in the gut. I knew the politics that would confront Oliza when she wanted to take a mate, but the casual assumption that Wyvern's Court was doomed was chilling.

"Perhaps the two cultures can keep from killing each other for a while," Spark stated, "but from birth to death they are as opposite as they can be. They can't exist together, and if they try to force it, the result can only be bloodshed."

Designed to be enemies.

There had to be a way to derail Araceli's plots, but I didn't know what it was. Not yet.

I tried to argue. "If they've come this far—"

"They've come this far only to find that they can't go any further," Spark interrupted. "The two cultures are able to co-exist temporarily—they've shown that—but asking them to combine like this land does is asking a snake and a bird to live together. Either the bird needs to give up the sky, or the snake needs to give up its earthen den. Both options demand too much."

Opal had returned to the doorway and was studying me. "I've realized where I've seen those marks before."

"Where?" I asked without thinking, but as I met his gaze, I instantly regretted it.

"On the Mercy," he said angrily, "when someone fights them. When they mindwalk and something goes wrong. On the Lady's chosen executioners."

Swiftly I realized what he had seen: some lingering vestige of magic from my moments with Hai in the *Ecl*. And I knew what he was afraid of. "No," I said quickly. "I know what you're thinking, but—"

"I don't care if you have Darien's magic on you," Opal challenged. "The only ones who come here with your power are from the Mercy, or are Pure Diamond. The Lady's hand, either way."

"I'm *not* working for Cjarsa or Araceli or any falcon," I protested. "I was born in Wyvern's Court—"

"Mongrel?" Maya interrupted.

"What? No," I answered, hastily enough to make even me flinch. When had I picked up *that* prejudice? "I tried to introduce myself earlier. My name is Nicias Silvermead—"

Gren rose to his feet so quickly that the stool he had been perched on toppled over, his mouth opening and closing in silent protest.

"Tar and feathers," Opal cursed. "Gren, you invited a *Wyvern* here? Why not invite the princess herself?"

Maya snarled, "Kel's son. Your mother is the Lady's Mercy and you have the gall to tell us—" She stopped when Gren caught her wrists, keeping her from moving toward me.

"Quiet!" Spark shrieked, sending the room into stunned silence. "Nicias, get out of here. *Now.* You're not welcome here." She started to reach forward as if to push me, but then recoiled.

I didn't feel the need to stay. I stepped outside, into rain that had started to fall heavily, and heard raised voices behind me.

Spark followed me out, making shooing motions. "Keep moving."

She kept pace as we crossed the market, and only when I was back on the doorstep of my own house did she speak again. "Maya has felt the Mercy's wrath before, as has Opal," she said. "Maya's punishment came at the hand of the woman you now call mother. One of them would have attacked you if you had stayed. You're just lucky they didn't make the connection to who your father is, and who his mother is."

"I wouldn't hurt any of you," I assured her. "Neither would my parents."

"Blood will tell, *sir,*" she said, with none of the respect usually associated with that title, but with a substantial amount of venom. "Mercy's blood and royal blood. You'll be as useless as the rest. I trust," she concluded coldly, "that we won't be seeing you again." Under her breath she added, "And you can be certain that you won't see us, either."

Shocked speechless, I could do nothing but retreat with whatever grace I had left. I entered my home, shaking Darien's illusion from myself as I crossed the threshold. How could I have thought, even for a moment, that I might find acceptance among falcons? I was too much a part of Wyvern's Court to be one of them.

No, that excuse was a lie. I was too much a part of Wyvern's Court to be happy on the island, but here among the exiles, I was too much a part of Ahnmik. *Mercy's blood and royal blood,* Spark had said.

You'll be as useless as the rest.

What had I done, really, besides run from Ahnmik? I had run home to Wyvern's Court, away from the place where I might have been able to make a difference.

It wasn't my fight.

The blood of royals may be strong with magic, but it's very thin when it comes to compassion.

I still needed to speak to my parents, yet I found myself drawn to Hai. If anything was my fight, she was, a cobra locked in a falcon's madness.

Arrogance, for me to think I could help her—but what choice did I have? Who was I, if not Nicias Silvermead, Wyvern of Honor, sworn to protect the royal houses of Wyvern's Court with every strength I possessed?

I put my hand on Hai's arm, closed my eyes and for the first time reached intentionally toward her nightmares.

The *Ecl'gah* in which Hai hid from the world had changed since I had left, but I was not sure whether the changes were for the better. Instead of the stark hues of last time, I found technicolor that dazzled the mind.

All around me were rolling fields of what seemed to be crystals as sharp as razors, which glowed in the light and bent in the intermittent wind like blades of grass. The sky was too vivid, a sunset gone mad with scarlet, amethyst and ginger, flames and waves swirling in no natural pattern. High above, a falcon circled, waiting, waiting to descend.

The cloying smell of sodden roses stuck to the back of my throat. The wind came from random directions at unexpected times, sometimes warm and sometimes frigid.

"Hai?" I called.

My own voice startled me. For all the disturbed beauty of this illusion, Hai had not woven sound into it. The wind was silent even as it danced past the same black castle I had seen too many times before in the distance.

I walked carefully through the crystal flora, to the moat that still circled the castle. The brimstone and serpents were gone, but the sparkling blue water steamed, and every now and then I glimpsed the back of some great scaled beast as it touched the surface of the water.

I could once again see Hai's silhouette looking down at me from the tallest tower.

"Hai?"

Why do you do this to me? Her voice was strained. *Why do you give me these dreams? Why must you wrap me with impossible illusions of wyverns and dancers and wings in the air?*

I staggered as the ground beneath me shifted. A raven screamed above me, and I looked up just in time to see the poor creature snapped from the air by a gyrfalcon. The falcon broke its prey's neck, scattering black feathers and blood to the ground.

Where they landed, the flowers and grass blackened as if brushed by a flame.

"It isn't impossible," I said to her, trying to turn away from the ugly sight. Again the illusion shifted, and baby cobras emerged where the raven's blood had fallen. "Hai, Wyvern's Court is real. I've seen—"

One of the cobras, now fully grown, reared up and hissed, flaring its hood.

If you believe in such bliss, Hai responded, *then I will pity you, poor hopeful boy. I pity you the fall you must soon face. Perhaps you should let the gentle void take you now, before you have to watch your world burn.*

"I'm not about to let it burn," I asserted. "And I'm not about to hide here from a difficult path."

She laughed, but the sound was like hot sand across my skin. "Nicias, you are already hiding. You walk in my world and tell me not to hide from my problems, but look what you have done. You are Araceli's only heir. She is not likely to give up on you so easily. Soon she will dare to enter the silent halls, and she will realize that you are not there. She will come to Wyvern's Court, and she will drag you back with her. Perhaps while she is here, she will execute the traitors who hide in the candle shop. Perhaps she will rid the world of your precious Oliza, whose reign she fears so much.

"You swore to defend Wyvern's Court, with your life if necessary," she said, accusingly. "Do not wait until it is too late."

The temperature dropped as if to match the sudden chill that had taken me as I heard the truth in her words.

No one has danced your future for you, have they? she asked. *Most fear the* sakkri'a'she. *It can burn one's mind, they say, but I spun that magic with almost every breath as I walked the streets of the white city. Let me see if I remember the steps . . .*

"Hai, wait—"

I was caught by her magic like a swallow taken by a hawk,

slammed from this *Ecl'gah* and onto the familiar green marble of Wyvern's Court's market plaza, where I held Oliza in my arms. My hands were marked with the blood from her wounds; she was cold and still. As I lifted my gaze, I saw that the land around us had been charred.

Oliza's body fell, listlessly, away from me as I stepped back in horror, wanting to flee the image.

"Hai!" I screamed. "This isn't real! Take it—"

Take it away? she asked me. *This may not be real, but trust me, sweet prince, it is a likely enough future.*

"Not one I will allow."

But you have no idea what causes it.

With that reply, she turned the vision, so that instead of being by Oliza, I knelt before Salem Cobriana. Near us, I could hear the shouting of a mob calling for blood, but my magic had pushed them back.

Too late.

Hai knelt next to me, but she did not lift her eyes to mine.

"Hai—"

Would you prefer a path less bloody? You could always walk this one . . .

I was gone from Wyvern's Court in an instant and then stood in one of the *yenna'marl* with Lily. When someone knocked at the door, I called out, "Come in," wondering what horror Hai had spun into this threat.

The man who opened the door knelt, not lifting his eyes as he spoke to us. "Sir, the Empress has requested your presence."

"We will be there shortly," Lily said when I hesitated. "We shouldn't keep Araceli waiting."

Then the vision ended, and I was back in Hai's illusion. I

could feel her agitation in the way the ice around me began to shiver.

What have you done, Nicias, that topples my Empress from her reign and puts your father's mother on the throne? Or, what have you not done?

Around me, I saw a million versions of myself, a million moments and possible futures. In some, I was Nicias of Ahnmik, heir to the Empress. In others, I stood beside Oliza in Wyvern's Court. In too many, I was left alone with the bodies of those slain.

Fail, Nicias . . . and the white towers fall. And the golden air of the wyvern's rule becomes a hell of silver ice. Swear to me, Nicias, that you will never betray your wyvern queen.

"You know I will not."

Swear it!

The creature in the moat lashed out, wrapping me in a serpentine body covered in blue and silver scales. I tried to retreat from Hai's mind, but found myself held fast; she had taken control of this moment, and I could only struggle feebly against the iron coils.

"I swear I will never betray Oliza."

The world shimmered as I spoke the words.

The creature set me down, and Hai spoke once more.

Then you must never become Ahnmik's prince. Know this, Nicias: There are already very few futures in which Oliza lives to rule—and there is not a single one in which you sit on the white throne and the wyvern survives to take her own.

What does that have to do with the Empress? I asked.

Araceli desires an heir before she betrays my Empress, Hai whispered, as if in a trance. *Right now, she believes that Darien lured you into Ecl. She believes that she can rescue you, and you will be grateful, and she will be able to win you back to her side.*

When my mother returns to Cjarsa's side, Araceli will be angry. When she next enters the Halls of shm'Ecl *and finds you gone and her plans in ruin, with Cjarsa's favored Mercy to blame, her fury will have no equal in this world. She will turn that anger upon Wyvern's Court as she seeks you, and when Cjarsa tries to calm her, Araceli will turn on my Empress and the white city will turn black. . . .*

If you hide, both our worlds will crumble.

You swore to defend Wyvern's Court, with your life if necessary, she repeated. *Now it becomes necessary.*

"Please, Nicias, do not do this to me," someone whispered, the words making Hai's illusion shiver. "Sweet Ahnmik, I have given you everything. Please, do not take my son from me."

My mother's prayers gently pulled me back from Hai's world. I was back in my home, at Hai's bedside, as if I had woken from a strange dream instead of the violent nightmare I was used to finding in Hai's realm.

I could still feel Oliza in my arms, her body limp and cold.

I looked up to find my mother and father both near me, my mother crying with relief. "We came to speak to you, and found you . . ." She gulped.

I lifted a hand to my mother's cheek, hating what I was about to do to her.

Despite her madness—or because of it—Hai was right. I couldn't stay here.

"Nicias, please, be careful," my father said. "When your mother told me that you were home, I thought it meant—"

"I am safe," I interrupted. I could not stand to hear his hopes when I was about to destroy them. "From my magic, at least. But I can't stay here. I was a fool to think I could.

Araceli will come looking for me sooner or later, and I cannot hide here when it puts all of Wyvern's Court in danger."

I looked at Hai. If she was right, I would not only be endangering my own world, but others' as well.

My father drew a deep breath. "What is it you intend to do?" he asked me.

"Go back." I could hardly say the words aloud. "Confront Araceli, and either convince her to let me go, or—" *Or what?* If I could not convince her to let me go, I would need to stay on Ahnmik to keep her from threatening Wyvern's Court. How long would it take for her manipulations and persuasion magics to soften my resolve and convince me that I had a place on the white throne of Ahnmik?

I asked my mother, "How true is a vision seen in a *sakkri'a'she*?"

She winced. "No vision seen in a *sakkri* is impossible at the time it is woven," she answered.

If that was the case, then there was still a possible future in which I sat on Ahnmik's throne—and, according to Hai, somehow led to Oliza's demise.

If Araceli would not let me go, then I had only one option: I would give myself to *Ecl*, before I could do more damage.

"Nicias," my mother said, perhaps seeing the dark resolve on my face, "a *sakkri* can be wrong."

"And it can also be right—and that is not a chance I can take. I will not endanger Oliza that way. I will return, if I can, but for now I must leave."

My father caught my arm as I turned to go, and I thought that he would argue with me. Instead, he hugged me. "You could not be our son and do less," he whispered. "Even if, right now, I wish you were a little less noble."

My mother added her blessing. "Ahnleh protect you . . . and bring you home again."

I stepped out my door, instinctively reaching to Oliza even though I knew she had no magic and would never hear me. *I will always be loyal to you. But right now, I must leave you.*

Somehow she did hear. I even felt her reply, faint as it was. *Nicias, what . . . no, I trust you. Fly well.*

I didn't have time to question what power allowed her to answer me, or whether perhaps the words were a gift of my own imagination, trying to comfort me. I changed shape, spread my wings and shot into the sky.

The island where I had rested with Lily was drowned in water when I flew over it; no stopping there. I didn't think I could pause even if I wished to. My heart was pounding with fear.

The flight was a battle through rain and wind that made every stroke of my wings heavier and tried to drive me into the sea.

The destination, I knew, might be worse.

CHAPTER 16

ONCE AGAIN I landed in Ahnmik's plaza, crumpling to the ground as I returned to human form and desperately tried to catch my breath. The city was dark at that hour, except for the *yenna'marl*, which reflected the blush of dawn that had not yet crept past the horizon.

I started toward the palace, but hesitated when around a corner in the road I heard the soft conversation of a trio of falcons who had not noticed my arrival.

"I swear it's true. She was wearing the Mercy's uniform," a young man said, his voice hushed. "And arguing with Syfka, loudly enough that everyone on the street could hear her."

"Cjarsa must be mad," another responded. Hastily she added, "Far be it from me to question my Empress's judgment, but to place a traitor back into her favor is . . ."

"Suicidal?" the third, another man, suggested. "I've heard some say that Cjarsa is all but lost to *Ecl* already. Maybe she hopes Darien will kill her before the void finishes the job."

Darien? Wanting to know more, I turned the corner, not anticipating the kind of reaction my presence would produce. All three falcons paled at seeing me and went to their knees.

The one who had called the Empress suicidal spoke swiftly, pleading, "Sir, forgive me for my rashly spoken words. I am only a simple man. The decisions of my royal house are surely beyond my understanding."

Their fear only made my own worse. If they were so terrified by being caught speaking as they had, what would I face when I spoke to Araceli?

"Stand up," I said. "Please, tell me—Darien is back with the Empress?"

"Yes, among her Mercy," the man answered. "She is working beside Lillian."

But they hated each other.

"Lily was part of Araceli's guard," I challenged, trying to work out this puzzle.

"The Heir dismissed Lillian," the woman explained.

Probably because she had failed to keep me from Darien.

And now they were working together, beside the Empress. What next?

"Where can I find Araceli at this hour?"

The man who had begged my forgiveness seemed very happy to be able to answer me. "She is meeting with Syfka, once again. You could wait for her in the forum of the palace; I understand she is supposed to see the Empress next, and the Mercy would not refuse admittance to Araceli's own grandson and heir."

Did I really want to do this?

No.

Did I have a choice?

No.

"Thank you," I said. They seemed startled that I would bother, and even more startled when I walked past them on my way to the palace without saying more.

I had not even reached the base of the palace when a pair of guards moved to flank me, shimmering with Pure Diamond power. Before I could speak to them, they broke formation, to allow a quartet of women and men to approach.

Each wore a slender blade on his or her left hip. Gauntlets graced their wrists—some leather, and some appearing to be snakeskin—and they wore vests of the same material over their looser clothing. Their wings gave them away as peregrine, and the way they dismissed the Pure Diamond who had brought me there gave them away as something else: Araceli's Mercy.

A line of sweat formed between my shoulder blades as I fought the instinct to flee. I faced them with no way to defend myself against what was to come.

"Welcome back to Ahnmik, sir," one of them greeted me. Her eyes were liquid cobalt and flashed with distaste. "The Empress and her heir are separately occupied at the moment. They asked us to detain you and ensure you do not wander off again."

It occurred to me that if these four had felt Lily's "punishment" as Darien had, they might have good reason to hate me. "I didn't mean for her to be hurt," I said, raising the topic that I feared was on their minds. "I didn't know—"

One of the men glared. "Don't worry, sir, Lillian is fine. We're always careful not to irreversibly damage one of our own."

"Follow us, please," another said impatiently.

I followed; I saw no choice, even though my stomach was twisting as if it would turn itself inside out. This was a group of trained fighters, well practiced in magics that I was only beginning to grasp. Even if I fought, I would have no place to go unless I settled things here first.

My parents had found leniency. Painful as it had been, they had received their desired banishment. I hoped I could do the same.

My heart was pounding as I was led to the Mercy's tower. I doubted that if Araceli still hoped to have me as her heir, she would want permanent physical damage done. How much freedom did the Mercy have with me?

The anger I saw in their eyes said they would use all they could.

I felt the air pressure build as we walked up the weathered stone staircase to the top of the tower. There were no windows here, and the only light was provided by silver marks that snaked along the walls.

A force hit me, and with it I stopped seeing, hearing, knowing.

I couldn't scream, even though the world around me seemed to twist, compressing my lungs and lashing my skin.

In the midst of this, I was blindsided by a sickening guilt for what I had caused to happen, not just to Lily, but to every person I had ever judged. I thought of Araceli and could not summon my fury. I could not summon my resolve or remember why I had made the decisions I had.

She was my father's mother, after all. She had offered me everything, and I had spat on it like an ignorant, ungrateful child.

Vemka'tair'ka'o'ha'nas ... Someone was cursing in my mind, sputtering, *Weakling fool, are you going to let them mind-walk through your brain until you may as well be one of them?*

I felt this angry presence fight back, startling the Mercy enough to let me slip momentarily from their grasp.

Ice sliced open my hands as I fell gratefully into the *Ecl'gah,* suddenly the sweetest place I had ever been. I wanted to sink into the ice and stay there, numb.

Someone kicked me viciously, flipping me onto my back as I let out a yelp.

"You stain my world, *ruin* it, and then have the gall to try to give up?" These words were followed by a string of harsher ones, coming from a female figure who was slowly edging into focus. "You invade my dreams and tell me I am a fool for staying here, but the first time you are tested, you hide yourself away and dare to stand before me as a *hypocrite.*"

She dragged me to my feet and pinned me against the cold, black walls of her palace.

"Hai." I blinked in surprise, staring into a pair of furious garnet eyes—the ones I had seen long ago in the forest.

She smacked me, and I couldn't help wondering if staying with the Mercy would have been better. "Someone is calling you. Get back there."

I shuddered. Maybe I *would* rather she kept hitting me.

"I *will* keep hitting you," she snarled. "Ecl wants you, Nicias. She wants her price for saving you, and that price might be hundreds of years, enough to destroy your mind completely. Unless you get out *now!*" More gently, she said, "The worst is over. Go back."

I swallowed hard, then forced myself to agree, with a condition to make it worthwhile. "Only if you will."

She cursed and shook her head. "It's been too long. I can't."

"Darien seems to think you can."

"My mother is a fool."

We hung in silence for a moment. Again I felt the tug of the void, so inviting, painless and . . .

"You must go back," she whispered. "Don't fall here."

"What do you care?" I challenged.

"Damn you," Hai whispered. "I have danced a thousand futures and lived a thousand lifetimes and all I have seen is ashes and ice. You are too—You don't belong here. You have things you need to do, out there. Go, Nicias, *please.*"

"Only if you will."

"Swear you'll go back, and I'll try." Her voice was soft and frightened, but the words were enough.

"I swear."

"Then I swear as well."

***

There was blood on the floor when I returned to the *Now*—my blood, from a dozen lacerations across my back and my hands.

There were two women standing above me: Darien and Lily, I realized with relief.

"He's ours now," Lily said, "until the Lady and her heir return."

Darien took my hand and pulled me to my feet, smiling a bit. "The Empress believes in keeping a serpent close so she can watch it." She added silently, *No better place for me.*

Lily regarded me with cool detachment. "You might say thank you."

"Thank you?" My voice broke in my dry, tight throat.

"They would have done worse," she said.

"Why . . . did you stop them?"

"Nostalgia, maybe. Believe me or don't, but I did care for you." She shook her head. "Forgive me for saying, *sir*, but I've recovered from the affliction."

Darien prevented me from replying. "Cjarsa wants to meet with you before Araceli returns. Can you walk?"

"I can walk." I was still dazed, but I recalled enough to say to Darien, *Hai saved me.*

She gave me a sharp look. *She spoke to you?*

She made me swear to return. If she would.

Darien paused, swaying with shock. *She said the words?*

I went over the conversation with her as we walked.

A vow spoken to royal blood will bind her to this world, Darien whispered in my mind when I was through. *She will try. And she . . . may succeed.*

We reached the door to the reception hall of the palace, and I felt both Lily and Darien hesitate.

"I do not know how the Lady will receive you," Lily told me. "She and Araceli have been . . . displeased with each other, lately. I do not know what Cjarsa wants from you."

We stepped inside with the care of ones crossing a battlefield.

"Nicias of Ahnmik, you stand before the Empress Cjarsa, she who rules the white towers, lady of moon and mountain, sun and sea." Lily and Darien knelt at the Lady's feet, and Lily continued, "Great lady, allow me to present Nicias of Ahnmik, Nicias Silvermead, mindwalker, *mana'Ecl*, son of the son of your heir and of Kel, once of the Indigo Choir and of your Mercy."

"Stand aside," Cjarsa said.

They obeyed, moving to the edge of the doorway, though Darien sent me a wry *She usually will not lie outright. I hate her and she knows it, but even I must respect her.*

I faced the Empress of this cold, white land, unable even to imagine what the next few minutes might hold.

CHAPTER 17

CJARSA WAS AN eerily beautiful woman, with skin like milk and hair the color of white gold. Her eyes were the same mercury as Darien's, and her lashes just dark enough to set them off, hints of gold in a porcelain face. She wore a gown of deep violet, and the color was striking against her pure fairness.

"Nicias Silvermead, she forgot to add your title Wyvern of Honor." Her voice was musical, as haunting as wind whistling through barren cliffs. "I believe your post as the wyvern princess's guard is the one you respect."

"That is true, lady."

"I am sorry about your rough reception," she said, though there was no regret in her voice. There was no emotion at all. "Araceli's chosen are rather cross with you. I have had to take Lillian into my own employ, as Araceli refuses to forgive her. Though, of course, if you choose to stay, you may have her join yours."

"I have no desire to stay."

She sighed, but again the emotion she tried to portray

seemed forced, as if she was not attached to this world enough to feel the way we mortals did.

"Oh, yes, I am far detached from this realm," she said, as if I had spoken my thought aloud. "In my youth I spent time in the void, too much time exploring the illusions of *Ecl*. Darien will never forgive me for not reaching in and saving her daughter. She knows that I could. But Ecl is a temptation too strong for me. I am already too weary of this realm."

I shivered involuntarily, glancing at Darien without meaning to. The gyrfalcon averted her gaze, jaw set. *Ignore me, Nicias. Speak to Cjarsa,* Darien commanded. *I do not know what she wants, but I do know that she is the only one with the power to keep you from Araceli.*

"Nicias, please sit," Cjarsa said, gesturing to a chair to her left. "There are things I need to discuss with you. A proposition I must make."

"Pardon me for being blunt, Lady," I said, "but after my other experiences in your land, I do not entirely trust your intentions."

She shrugged. "Sit, listen. I am not holding you, and I do not plan to. You know too much already about incidents that should have been forgotten in the past. Since our history seems to have proven that the truth has a way of finding the light, it seems best to end this problem here not by stripping that knowledge from your mind but by tempering it with understanding. Listening is not going to hurt you." She glanced at Darien. "We both know that my less-than-loving Darien will warn you if I lie or try to persuade you magically. Her candor is unusual in this land, and one of the reasons I asked her back to my side."

Darien nodded.

"I am listening," I said.

Cjarsa smiled a little, her expression still somehow cold. "I know that Darien has told you of our actions regarding Kiesha's and Alasdair's peoples. While I may not always approve of Araceli's *methods,* her motivations—in this case, at least—were correct. If you had lived through the early days after the Dasi split, you would understand the necessity of what was done. You only hate it because you were raised among those you see as most harmed."

"Are you going to argue that they weren't most harmed?" I asked, trying to keep my words even and my head clear of the anger that was surfacing.

"The magic of Ahnmik balances itself," Cjarsa explained. "Ahnmik is the energy of stillness and silence. It will bring one to *Ecl* when it is too strong, and he succumbs to sleep.

"Anhamirak's magic is different. It is a magic of wildfires, tornadoes, thunderstorms, bloodshed. Yes, she represents freedom and beauty, but she also represents chaos. When her magic is out of control, it burns. First it will burn out the mind of the user, and then it will destroy what is around him.

"Back in Maeve's coven, Ahnmik and Anhamirak's powers balanced each other. Kiesha and I worked side by side. When the serpiente forced us out, they destroyed that balance. Their magic became as unsteady as ours, but theirs had the power to destroy more than ours ever could.

"When we created the avians, it was more than a way to keep the serpiente from remembering Anhamirak's magic. Avians are *part* of the serpiente magic, a part we removed but could never destroy. That is why, though they have hated each other for ages, they are drawn together. Each is the missing half of the other's magic. When the pair breeds together, the magic joins in the child. Likely, that first child's magic will never awaken. Even if it does, it will be stunted and sluggish. But over generations . . .

"If Oliza takes the throne, her heirs *will* have Anhamirak's magic. It will destroy first them, then their people, and quite possibly the rest of their world as well, until stopped by the only thing that *can* balance Anhamirak: lack of existence. Lack of anything left to burn."

She shifted her gaze from one of the swirling patterns of magic on the walls to me. "Can you understand, Nicias?"

Could I? Did I?

Perhaps the ends *did* justify Cjarsa's means, but even if they did, what was there to do? I would still not be part of an effort to launch the avians and the serpiente back into war. Nor could I refuse to let Oliza come to the throne where she belonged.

I was no prince, no king; these decisions should never have belonged to me.

Cjarsa continued, "We designed the avians to be opposite from all the serpiente believed in, so that even if they were not at war, they could not become one race again. Neither civilization will bend; the only way your Wyvern's Court could truly combine them is to entirely destroy the culture of one. That was intentional. Perhaps they do not need war, but they must not be allowed to keep forcing this merge, either."

"I am not loyal to you, or to Araceli, or to Ahnmik," I answered. "I have already refused to be part of an uprising in your land, so you need not fear that from me, but never will I betray my queen-to-be by helping sabotage the people of Wyvern's Court. So, please, tell me plainly what you want with me."

"How far does your loyalty stretch?" Cjarsa challenged.

"Even in Wyvern's Court, there are many who are wary of the time when Oliza will come to the throne. No matter who she chooses, there will be those who hate her mate enough to consider killing him, and maybe your queen as well. And after that, will your loyalty stretch so far that you would let a wyvern's blood destroy the world she rules?"

"I find it difficult to believe that you could perform a magic strong enough to rend the serpiente of half their power and give it to another race," I said defiantly, "and yet you cannot do anything to protect this potential child from herself."

"I am no longer the young fool who once dove recklessly into *Ecl* and warped Fate herself to her will," Cjarsa sighed, her voice distant once again. "I have neither the strength nor the power to do such a thing a second time."

"Araceli bound my parents' magic so that it would not destroy them," I said, thinking aloud. "If the child showed magic, couldn't it too be bound?"

"Nicias, it has been many long years since I have been able to feel a summer wind on my skin, or hear the music of a choir, or savor fresh fruit. I can see Ahnmik's power, and so I can control it, but I am blind to Anhamirak's warmth. Asking me to bind her power is asking me to paint in red and blue a sunrise that I can see only in gray. I could rip the magic from the child entirely, but I could never control it otherwise."

"If that is the only way you will let Oliza's child live, the people of Wyvern's Court could live without magic. They always have."

Cjarsa shook her head sadly. "The serpiente, the avians, they are creatures of Anhamirak's fire. They may not use it consciously, but it is what gives them their scales and their feathers. It is what makes them immune to the plagues and weaknesses that infect humans. If you take it from them, they will die. That is what *am'haj,* the poison Araceli designed and gave to the avians to help them fight the serpiente, does: rekindle the dormant magic that long ago split Anhamirak's power between Kiesha and Alasdair, and allow that ancient spell to destroy what is left."

I lay my palms flat against the wall, thinking of all the lives that had been lost. There had to be a way to solve this that did not involve the destruction of Wyvern's Court and a return to the horrors of the past.

I jumped as the doors to the hall slammed open. As I turned toward the violent intrusion, I saw Darien and Lily draw their weapons, moving between Cjarsa and the interlopers. Though I would have sworn that the four of us had been alone, two more guards appeared as if they had melted from the walls.

Araceli stood with her wings held tightly to her back in the way of an avian warrior. Syfka stood to her left; two of Araceli's Mercy were to her right.

"This is low, Cjarsa," Araceli spat. "You stay in your palace hall all day and night, drifting almost as badly as the *shm'Ecl.* When you emerge, first you take traitors under your wing—traitors who should be shorn of their wings for treason and worse crimes. And now you try to turn my own blood—"

"You are looking for an excuse for your uprising," Cjarsa interrupted. "Nicias was never loyal to you; do not accuse me of turning him against you."

"I can accuse your precious Darien of that crime," Araceli answered hotly. "And we all know to whose hand she has always belonged."

Darien laughed, never allowing her blade to waver or her attention to falter from Araceli and her guards.

If this became a battle, who would I fight for? Would I fight, or could I flee?

Araceli wants Cjarsa dethroned. She accuses Cjarsa of being an idle Empress over a stagnant land, Darien whispered to me. *She wants to take power, and build Ahnmik in the great image she sees. She wanted you for her heir, a loyal addition to her power after she disposes of her obstacles.*

Obstacles like Cjarsa.

I jumped as Cjarsa spoke to me, her voice like ice. *Araceli craves power; she has no understanding of balance. And it looks as if she has turned my Syfka against me now, as well.*

She spoke on this point. "Syfka, beautiful aplomado, has she wooed you to her madness as well? Has your time off Ahnmik stained you so badly that you cannot see the danger in Araceli's plans?"

Araceli did not allow Syfka to answer. "Your aplomado was the one who first considered destroying you."

I saw Darien frown. Her command was like a shove. *Look at Araceli, Nicias, and tell me what you see. Araceli is power hungry, but she has never been insane. If she fights here, even if she kills Cjarsa, she will fall.*

When Darien said *look,* she meant with magic. Cjarsa and Araceli continued to argue, the Empress's voice getting softer as Araceli's grew louder, but I ignored all that as I tentatively reached out to my father's mother.

Movement.

I stumbled as a wave of Darien and Lily's magic crossed the room, knocking back the two Mercy that Araceli had brought with her. I reached out at the same time that Araceli retaliated. Her magic slammed into me like a tsunami, forcing the breath from my lungs.

As the power flooded over me, I recognized the pattern

hidden in it. The design was infinitely complex, woven through thoughts that Araceli had long harbored, but on the most basic level, it was the same as the persuasion magics Lily had once used on me.

They were well disguised, so subtle and yet so tightly wound that their creation had surely taken years, decades perhaps. Araceli was blind to them the way I had been blind to Lily's. Cjarsa could not delve deeply into this power without drowning, and so she must not have seen it. And the Mercy could not read the lines because they seemed to have been put in place by one of royal blood. Darien only suspected their existence.

I threw the knowledge at Cjarsa and her four guards and felt them react. The two in back had gone to Cjarsa's side to defend her, but Darien and Lily moved forward. When Darien knelt and touched my brow, I shuddered, drawing breath for the first time since I had fallen.

"Would you kill your own kin to win this fight?" Darien asked softly, eyes lifted to Araceli. As she forced me to breathe and my heart to beat, I felt her using my power to read the magic Araceli wore.

Araceli shuddered. For the moment of indecision, the persuasion magics wavered.

Suddenly I made the connection.

Darien had said that Araceli would not survive if she forced this fight. If she and the Empress both fell, Syfka would be next in line—unless I stayed as Araceli's heir. No wonder Syfka had wanted me gone and had "helped" my father to flee years before. She had been planning to destroy both royals for years, but new ones kept appearing.

Lily walked past Darien. I caught a glimpse of a peculiar magic, which could be only the bond among the Mercy, being funneled into Lily. It left three of Cjarsa's Mercy all but defenseless, but Lily as strong as all four combined.

Lily spoke to Syfka, as quietly as Darien had, "Beautiful aplomado, there's no need for you to fall with the heir."

Syfka's wings snapped open, aggressive. "Drop your weapon, Lillian," she commanded.

"I guard the Empress first," Lily answered, "and her house second. You are part of that house, and I hesitate to fight you unless I must. So I ask you, stand down."

Araceli must have felt the strands of Syfka's magic and was unraveling them slowly, because she was shuddering like one coming out of a deep, cold sleep. She was watching Syfka warily, too, and I knew that she had also realized why the aplomado had worked so hard to send Araceli's heirs away.

"My lady," Syfka began. She never finished.

Lily and Araceli both turned on the traitor at the same time. No physical weapon was ever used, but Syfka crumpled, her wings dissolving back into her body. Magic wrapped around her, a net to hold her in place.

"Nicias Silvermead," Cjarsa addressed me as her guards hauled the still form up. "You've already seen more of our quarrel than you should have."

Araceli opened her mouth to protest, then shook her head, averting her gaze. "Lady . . ." She did not say more.

"Say goodbye to Sebastian's son, Araceli. Nicias must return to his own people." Cjarsa looked back at me. "He is an intelligent child. When the time comes for him to choose whether to follow his queen or not, he will choose well."

I would have to tell Oliza what I knew and give her Cjarsa's warnings, but she was my queen, and it was not my place to make decisions for her.

Hopefully I could get her to delay the day she would

choose her mate and take the throne. In the meantime, I would practice what I had learned from Darien. Cjarsa might be too lost to *Ecl* to touch Mehay, but I was not. I hoped that by the time Oliza reigned, I might have the control to protect any child of hers from itself.

Araceli sighed and knelt beside me.

"May I leave now?" I asked. "With your blessing?"

She hesitated. Then she kissed my forehead and withdrew the magic she had harmed me with.

"One last word before you go, Nicias," she answered. "Oliza is very fond of you, true? I know she sees in you a kindred spirit."

I swallowed tightly. "I like to think that is true. We have been friends most of our lives."

"Be careful that someday soon that interest doesn't turn into more than friendship," Araceli warned. "I'm sure you understand how deadly it would be for you to take her as your mate. Adding falcon blood to a wyvern's would be a poor idea. But not so much a problem, as both the serpiente and the avians would kill you before they would allow you to stand as king."

Of *that* I had no doubt. "I love Oliza in many ways, Lady, but I have no desire to be her king. If I wanted to rule, I could stay here." That would not change, though Araceli's warning had made me think of something else. "But if in another world it was possible for falcons and serpiente to be together, wouldn't our magics balance each other, as they once did before Maeve's coven split?"

"Perhaps," Araceli admitted. "Perhaps the child would be able to wield both magics, without losing control of either. Imagine the kind of power she could have, and combine it with the right to reign she would inherit. Neither you nor your mate would have the strength to control her, and absolute power is as dangerous as Ahnmik's ice and Anhamirak's fire combined."

"Absolute power like you and Cjarsa have in this land?" I asked.

Araceli looked amused as she answered, "I know what you think of our realm, *ra'o'ra*. Go now, Nicias. If you return to Ahnmik in the future, you will always be greeted as my heir, whether you choose to stay for an hour, for a year, or forever. Cjarsa will not allow me to hold you here, so I will leave the decision up to you. Perhaps if the offer remains open, you will one day accept. Until then, fly with grace, fly with purpose, fly with strength."

✳✳✳

When I returned to Wyvern's Court, I paused only to change my clothes quickly and wash the blood from my skin before I sought Oliza.

She was sitting on a grassy knoll with her cousin Salem, and a couple of their friends. Marus was also sitting with them, close enough to Oliza for his hand to touch hers.

She was so young, I realized as I approached her. What I had seen and learned on Ahnmik made me feel ancient.

I had removed all magic from myself, so the crowd recognized me as I approached. Oliza smiled when she saw me.

I tried to smile in return.

"Are you finally back for good?" she asked. "I have been worried about you."

"I think so," I answered. "And I have permission from

both Cjarsa and Araceli to be here, so I am not a danger to anyone."

I hope.

"Welcome home, then."

She stood to hug me and invited me to sit with them as she returned to Marus's side. There was so much more I wanted to say, but there would be too many people listening.

Hopefully later would still be soon enough.

✳✳✳

I returned again to my home, where I checked in on Hai.

She lay on her side on the guest room bed, one hand tucked beneath her head, looking as peaceful as I had ever seen her, but as pale and still as ever.

I felt a crush of disappointment, though I tried to push it away. Darien had given me hope, but what had I expected? I started to turn away, and then I noticed a *melos* and a small open box that had been set on the bedside table. Both were from the collection of belongings I had taken from my mother's room.

Someone sighed behind me. *You're here. I suppose that means I must cease dreaming that I am not.*

I turned back to see Hai pushing herself into a seated position. Her face was falcon fair, her hair dark as *Ecl,* and her eyes the deathly still pools of blood that I had looked into weeks before, when I had fallen in the woods. Only as she leaned back against the headboard did I realize that she had taken down her wings. She pulled her knees up to her chest as if she was cold.

She looked very fragile in this world.

"Welcome back," I said to her.

Your wyvern pretended to be glad that I have "recovered," but she is a poor liar compared to a royal falcon. She peered at the possessions that had drawn my attention a moment before. *A father killed within days of my conception, and a mother who would rather have vengeance than raise her own daughter. Such a legacy I am honored to have.*

She opened one of her hands, to reveal one of the Cobriana signet rings.

I suppose it was my father's, Hai whispered, slipping it on just long enough to see that it was far too large for her. She took it off and closed it in her palm for a moment. When she tried it on again, it fit as if crafted for her hand.

The casual use of power unnerved me no less than her idly adorning herself with the symbol of the royal serpiente house. What had I done?

You are the one who woke me, my prince, she reminded me. *A'she'hena; the rest is in the future's hands.*

✳✳✳

o'Mehay
shmah'Mehay-hena'keyika
ka-shmah'Mehay-jacon'itil
a'quean'enae

But he who dances with Mehay, he is lost—
For he who dances with Mehay cannot leave the dance
And will face the fire.

Nesera
So dance.

About the Author

Amelia Atwater-Rhodes grew up in Concord, Massachusetts. Born in 1984, she wrote her first novel, *In the Forests of the Night*, praised as "remarkable" *(Voice of Youth Advocates)* and "mature and polished" *(Booklist)*, when she was thirteen. She has since published *Demon in My View*, *Shattered Mirror*, and *Midnight Predator*, all ALA Quick Picks for Young Adults; *Hawksong*, a *School Library Journal* Best Book of the Year and a *Voice of Youth Advocates* Best Science Fiction, Fantasy, and Horror selection; and *Snakecharm*.